JANE AUSTEN'S
~EMMA~

AWESOMELY AUSTEN

Illustrated by Églantine Ceulemans

JANE AUSTEN'S
EMMA

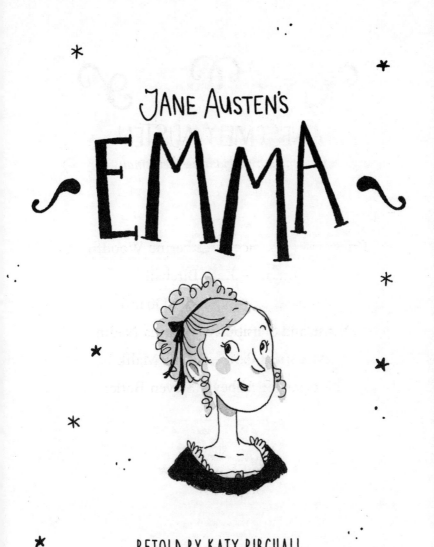

RETOLD BY KATY BIRCHALL
ILLUSTRATED BY ÉGLANTINE CEULEMANS

HODDER

First published in Great Britain in 2019 by Hodder and Stoughton

1 3 5 7 9 10 8 6 4 2

Text copyright © Katy Birchall, 2019
Illustrations copyright © Églantine Ceulemans, 2019

The moral right of the author has been asserted.

A CIP catalogue record for this book
is available from the British Library.

ISBN 978 1 444 95065 6

Typeset in Bembo
Printed and bound in Great Britain by Clays Ltd, Elcograf S.p.A

The paper and board used in this book
are made from wood from responsible sources.

Hodder Children's Books
An imprint of
Hachette Children's Group
Part of Hodder and Stoughton
Carmelite House
50 Victoria Embankment
London EC4Y 0DZ

An Hachette UK Company
www.hachette.co.uk

www.hachettechildrens.co.uk

Emma, by Jane Austen, was first published in 1815.

This was the Regency era – a time when English society was sharply divided by wealth and women were expected to marry young.

The heroine of this story, Emma, might have some things in common with modern readers, but she lived in a very different world.

You can find out more about Jane Austen and what England was like in 1815 at the back of this book!

MAIN CHARACTERS

MR WOODHOUSE
Emma's father. Lives at Hartfield House in Highbury village.

(JOHN AND GEORGE'S PARENTS)

MRS ISABELLA KNIGHTLEY
Emma's older, married sister. Lives in London.

MR JOHN KNIGHTLEY
Emma's brother-in-law. Lives in London with Isabella.

MISS EMMA WOODHOUSE
Our heroine! Lives at Hartfield House and is beloved by all the residents of Highbury village.

THE KNIGHTLEY CHILDREN
Emma's nephews and nieces, including baby Emma (named after her aunt).

MR GEORGE KNIGHTLEY
Emma's best friend, lives at Donwell Abbey in Highbury village. A little bit older than Emma.

MRS BATES
The mother of Miss Bates, and grandmother of Miss Jane Fairfax. Poor in comparison with most of the wealthy characters in this story.

(JANE'S MOTHER)

MISS BATES
The resident chatterbox of Highbury village. Aunt of Miss Jane Fairfax. Poor in comparison with most of the wealthy characters in this story.

MISS JANE FAIRFAX
The niece of Miss Bates. An orphan who has been brought up by wealthy guardians, the Campbells, and has lived away from Highbury for a long time. A similar age to Emma.

MR WESTON
The new husband of Emma's old governess. Lives in Highbury village.

MRS WESTON
Emma's former governess, who was called Miss Taylor before getting married. Lives in Highbury village with her new husband.

MR FRANK CHURCHILL
Mr Weston's son from his first marriage. Brought up by his aunt (Mrs Churchill) after his own mother died and has lived away from Highbury for a long time. A similar age to Emma.

MISS HARRIET SMITH
Emma's great friend. As a child, her mysterious, unknown parents placed her in a boarding school in Highbury village run by Mrs Goddard. She now helps Mrs Goddard run the school. A similar age to Emma.

MR ELTON
The vicar of Highbury village. A little bit older than Emma.

MR MARTIN
A farmer. Lives in Highbury village. A little bit older than Emma.

CHAPTER ONE

Emma Woodhouse was beautiful, clever and rich, and had reached the age of twenty-one with very little to trouble her along the way.

But on the evening of her governess Miss Taylor's wedding, Emma felt very troubled indeed. Her father had fallen asleep in his favourite armchair after dinner and silence had descended upon the room but for the crackling fire and Mr Woodhouse's gentle snores. Emma thought glumly: with Miss Taylor gone, who was she to talk to now?

She was very happy for Miss Taylor – now Mrs Weston – but having spent sixteen years in her company, Emma would miss her dearly. She had been more of a friend than a governess. Emma couldn't recollect ever hearing one strict word from Miss Taylor and knew that, though Miss Taylor had been fond of Emma's older sister Isabella too, she'd always had a soft spot for the youngest Miss Woodhouse. In Miss Taylor's eyes, Emma could do no wrong, which had been very convenient when it came to getting her own way ...

Emma's mother had died when she was too young to remember her, but Miss Taylor was always there to look after Emma when she fell ill, to laugh with her as she concocted some mischievous scheme, and to speak to as soon as a thought popped into her head. So, Emma had never felt a lack of motherly affection. Even when Isabella got married and left Highbury, their countryside village, to move to London, Emma hadn't felt left behind. She happily took to being mistress of Hartfield House, gently guided in daily matters by her governess. It had been, quite simply, a perfect situation.

Emma sighed, smoothing the crinkles on her gown, before lifting her chin defiantly. She must bear this change in an admirable and elegant manner and not sit around moping like a sulky child. After all, the marriage had been Emma's idea in the first place.

She was just congratulating herself on bringing together the new Mr and Mrs Weston when a pot of tea was brought in by the housemaid and her father woke with a start.

'Poor Miss Taylor!' he declared, before pulling his blanket further up his lap. 'Such a pity for her to have been taken away from Hartfield. She would have been much happier spending the rest of her life with us here.'

Emma smiled. Mr Woodhouse had always despised change of any kind.

'Papa, *Mrs Weston* has a house of her own now and a very generous, agreeable husband. She could not stay here and put up with me for ever, as you very well know.'

Mr Woodhouse harrumphed. 'Hartfield is three times the size of her new house. Poor Miss Taylor, she will be quite put out.'

'But she doesn't live far. We will see Mr and Mrs Weston very often, as they are sure to visit us as much as we visit them,' Emma said cheerily.

'It is too far for me to walk,' Mr Woodhouse protested. 'I shall catch cold.'

'No one would expect you to walk, Papa.' Emma

laughed, shaking her head. 'We would take the carriage, of course.'

'The carriage is most inconvenient for the horses,' her father grumbled, leaving Emma to smile into her cup of tea.

Mr Woodhouse was a nervous gentleman in a constant state of worry about falling ill. He couldn't quite understand why any person of good sense would go to the trouble of leaving their cosy household to venture outdoors. In his mind, social occasions outside of Hartfield were tiresome and often put one at great risk of indigestion or other such alarming ailments. Though he generally delighted in guests coming to visit him, he found hosting large dinner parties in particular a tense affair. Not only might they make him late to bed, but there was also the matter of checking the menu through with the cook beforehand at least four times, so that he was sure no dangerously rich foods might be served to his guests. In the eyes of Mr

Woodhouse, there was no greater crime in the world than serving a dish that might bring about tummy ache.

One of Mr Woodhouse's favourite visitors, a young, dark-haired gentleman, entered the room just as Emma was considering whether a game of backgammon might work to lift her father's spirits.

'Mr Knightley!' Mr Woodhouse said warmly. 'How kind of you to call in so late. Come warm yourself by the fire before you catch cold. The walk must have been damp and dreary!'

'Not at all,' Mr Knightley replied with a bow of his head and a knowing smile to Emma. 'It is a mild, moonlit night and made for a very pleasant walk.'

Mr George Knightley was the brother of John, who had married Emma's sister, Isabella. As such, Mr Knightley was always welcome at Hartfield and came by often. He lived at Donwell Abbey, an estate only a mile away, and took great pleasure in spending quiet evenings with Mr Woodhouse and his daughter.

Having just returned from paying his brother and sister-in-law a visit in London, Mr Knightley patiently answered Mr Woodhouse's questions about Isabella and the children, before the conversation was steered back to the day's events.

'Did everyone behave at the wedding?' Mr Knightley asked, sitting back in his chair. 'Pray, tell me who cried the most?'

'It is a sad occasion,' Mr Woodhouse said gravely. 'Poor Miss Taylor.'

'Not "poor Miss Taylor", for she will surely find much happiness in moving from the position of governess to having her own home. At any rate, she now has only her husband to worry about,' Mr Knightley noted, his eyes twinkling playfully at Emma, 'rather than two here at Hartfield.'

'Especially when one of us at Hartfield is so fanciful and difficult.' Emma grinned. 'That is what you are longing to add, is it not Mr Knightley?'

'Yes, it is true,' Mr Woodhouse sighed. 'I can be fanciful and difficult.'

'I did not mean you, Papa!' Emma laughed. 'You must know I meant myself. Mr Knightley loves to tease me about all my faults.'

'True friends would never waste time flattering one another,' Mr Knightley replied with a smile, knowing full well that he was the only person in the whole village who saw any faults in Emma Woodhouse. 'You must be very pleased, Emma, to see your dear governess so happily married.'

'More so than anyone else, because it was I who made the match myself. Four years ago, I decided Mr Weston and Miss Taylor must marry, despite everyone in Highbury declaring Mr Weston would never marry again. What a success!'

'Success? You make it sound as though *you* have brought about this marriage entirely,' Mr Knightley said, shaking his head at her.

'And so I did!' Emma declared proudly. 'If I hadn't encouraged Mr Weston's visits and promoted his character when needed, we might not have had a wedding today.'

'It was a lucky guess,' Mr Knightley said, a smile creeping across his lips. 'No doubt you did more harm than good with your meddling.'

'Emma is very generous,' Mr Woodhouse interjected, not really paying attention to the conversation. 'But, my dear, if you did bring about the marriage today, I ask that you bring about no others. Marriage only serves to break up one's family circle and exposes us to the very great risk of sugar-filled wedding cake!'

'One more match, Papa,' Emma said, sitting up a little taller. 'I am determined to find a wife for Mr Elton.'

'The vicar?'

'Yes, Papa. When Mr Elton joined Mr and Mrs Weston's hands in marriage today, I could see that he would very much like to have the same thing happen for him.'

'Instead of finding him a wife, perhaps you might invite him for dinner,' Mr Woodhouse suggested. 'That will be a much better thing for him. Mr Knightley will agree with me.'

'I do, sir.' Mr Knightley laughed at Emma's stubborn expression. 'Let us leave poor Mr Elton to find his own wife. A man of twenty-seven doesn't need any help in such matters.'

Emma smiled in reply and let the conversation move on, but her mind was already busy plotting. Mr Knightley was greatly mistaken. Emma Woodhouse was quite sure that, when it came to love, men needed all the help they could get.

And she was the perfect person for the job.

CHAPTER TWO

'My dear Emma, I have such good news.'

Mrs Weston had barely sat down in the Hartfield drawing room before making such an animated declaration. Emma leaned in towards her friend eagerly. She was always keen for news and they only had a few minutes to talk alone before the rest of her dinner guests arrived.

'We have had a letter from Frank Churchill,' Mrs Weston confided, as her husband went to join Mr Elton, the vicar, and Mr Woodhouse on the other side of the room.

'I have heard of this letter,' Emma confessed. (This could come as no surprise to Mrs Weston, who knew only too well how quickly gossip spread in the village of Highbury.) 'Do not keep me in suspense of the content any longer! What did the famous Frank Churchill write to his new step-mother to say? I hope he wished you and his father good wishes on your marriage?'

'That he did,' Mrs Weston assured her. 'But the good news I wish to share is that he writes in the hope of visiting us soon! How I long for him to come here to Highbury and meet us all. Do you think he really shall?'

Emma hesitated as she considered her answer.

She certainly *hoped* that Frank Churchill would come at last to Highbury. Not only would it be the proper thing for a son to do on his father's second marriage, but there was also a rumour of his being a fine young gentleman, and Emma wondered, for no other reason than mere curiosity, as to whether that was so.

This generous rumour of Frank Churchill's

appearance and character had been started by the only person who had actually met him – his father. Frank was the son of Mr Weston and his first wife, Miss Churchill. She had passed away when Frank was a boy and it had been thought best that Frank be brought up by his wealthy aunt and uncle, Mr and Mrs Churchill – Frank's surname was changed and he became the Churchills' heir.

Though Mr Weston had taken great pleasure in visiting his son over the years, Frank was yet to visit his father at his home in Highbury. Now elderly and prone to illness, Mrs Churchill was particularly attached to Frank and it was well-known that he was hardly allowed to leave her side. Mr Weston and all of his friends dearly hoped that Mrs Churchill might change her mind and let Frank introduce himself to their society.

'Well, dear?' Mrs Weston prompted Emma, who had become lost in her thoughts as she mused on whether Frank Churchill had sideburns and if so,

FRANK Churchill

Stylishly attired

Excellent Horseman

Aristocratic Character

Writes polite & refined letters

Admires fine music & dancing

whether they were long or short. 'Do you think it is silly of me to hope he will visit?'

Emma smiled and took her friend's hand in hers. 'I think it would be silly of you *not* to have hope that he should visit. Ah' – Emma paused on seeing four ladies enter the drawing room, just arrived – 'Mrs and Miss Bates are here. And Mrs Goddard.'

'Who is that pretty young lady with Mrs Goddard?' Mrs Weston asked curiously, watching the girl enter the grand drawing room shyly, gazing around her in awe.

'That,' Emma began, rising to her feet, 'is Miss Harriet Smith. Mrs Goddard wrote to me today asking if she may bring her to the dinner. Come, let us welcome her.'

Emma was delighted to meet Miss Smith. She knew her by sight, having seen her trailing after Mrs Goddard to church. Mrs Goddard ran a boarding school and Harriet Smith had been one of her students. Now, at seventeen, she still lived there and helped Mrs Goddard with the children.

There was some mystery surrounding the girl. No one knew her parents, nor their profession or rank in society. But within minutes of meeting Miss Smith, Emma decided that her father must be a gentleman. She was such a sweet girl, and so charmingly grateful to be dining in high society with Miss Emma Woodhouse, that Emma felt certain she must come from a family of good sense.

'It is so kind of you to let me come tonight, Miss Woodhouse,' Harriet Smith gushed later that evening, hoping very much she was saying the right sort of thing. So esteemed was Miss Emma Woodhouse that Harriet had been unable to eat all day at the prospect of being allowed to meet her. Not one thing ... except lunch and two tea buns ...

'It is a pleasure to meet you, Miss Smith,' Emma replied, coming to stand opposite her, next to Mrs and Miss Bates.

'Oh, Miss Woodhouse! The apple tart!' Miss Bates exclaimed, before Harriet could respond. 'I have always said that no apple tart beats the apple tart served here at Hartfield. How fortunate we are to taste such a tart! And with such custard! Apple tart is quite my favourite tart, wouldn't you agree, Mother?'

Mrs Bates did not respond. An elderly widow who had spent years listening to her daughter's shrill, long-winded compliments of everyone and everything, Mrs Bates had long since decided that the best thing to do in her old age was to go deaf, and so she had.

'What a pretty picture on the wall there, Miss Woodhouse,' Miss Bates continued happily, moving swiftly on from the subject of apple tart. 'Did you

paint it? For you are such a talented painter! What a blessing to be able to come here to Hartfield. So obliging of you, Miss Woodhouse, to let us join you! Do you paint, Miss Smith? Or do you prefer music? For Miss Woodhouse is so elegant at the pianoforte! Miss Woodhouse, you remember my niece, Jane Fairfax, she adores to play. How I should like to hear her play! Oh! Look at Mr Elton over there! How well he stands! Mother, we must go and tell him how much we enjoyed his sermon. Such brilliant speaking! So clear! So distinct! I do think his hair is very well-combed. Don't you? We must tell him so!'

Emma smiled at Miss Bates as she eagerly led her mother towards the unsuspecting gentleman on the other side of the room.

Everyone in Highbury was fond of Miss Bates, for nothing could dampen her spirits. She had never been rich, clever or handsome and, unmarried with no prospects, she devoted her life to caring for her mother. And yet, she thought herself so blessed. She had such wonderful friends and such generous neighbours, and had never met anyone in her entire life who had one flaw to speak of.

Emma watched in amusement as Miss Bates flattered Mr Elton so much on his heavenly manner of speaking that his cheeks flushed quite pink.

'Miss Smith,' Emma began, 'I find myself agreeing with Miss Bates's observation, how well Mr Elton looks! Would not you agree?'

'Oh yes, Miss Woodhouse, certainly.' She nodded, quite determined to agree with everything Miss Woodhouse said.

Emma was satisfied with her answer and did not push the matter further.

It was clear to her that Harriet Smith, though naturally graceful, was in great need of someone to improve her in both knowledge and elegance. In an instant, Emma decided she would take on such a role and guide her into better society. With Emma's kind influence, Miss Smith's qualities would be sure to be noticed by all the right people. And, if Emma had her way, one right person in particular.

Emma could not help but glance at Mr Elton, who caught her eye and smiled.

How funny, Emma thought as she smiled back graciously, *he has no idea that he is soon to fall madly in love!*

CHAPTER THREE

'I do beg your pardon, Harriet, I'm not entirely sure I heard you right just now,' Emma said, blinking in surprise. 'Did you say Mr Martin gave you a *cow*?'

Harriet nodded cheerfully. 'Yes indeed, Miss Woodhouse. Although, I suppose, he did not give me her as such, in that I have nowhere to keep a cow. Fancy, me keeping a cow in Mrs Goddard's parlour!' Harriet burst into a fit of giggles at such a thought. 'No, what happened was that I said that one of the cows on his farm was very pretty – in a cow sort of way – and Mr Martin declared that as I liked it so much, then it should be my cow!'

'I see,' Emma said, startled to see that her friend suddenly had a dreamy look on her face and wasn't paying attention to where she was walking. 'Do watch that tree, dear!'

'Oh goodness.' Harriet laughed, veering back on to the path and narrowly avoiding what might have been a most unfortunate collision. 'Sorry, Miss Woodhouse, I fell into quite a daze.'

Oh dear. This would not do. Emma sighed as they continued their walk, wondering how best to tackle this unforeseen challenge.

Her acquaintance with Harriet Smith had grown since their introduction at Hartfield. Harriet could not believe her luck – Miss Emma Woodhouse had not only shaken her hand at the party, but had written to her the very next morning inviting her to join her as a walking companion! It was too wonderful to be believed! Since then, the two ladies had enjoyed several walks together and on these walks both grown in affection for one another.

EMMA

Miss Woodhouse was, in Harriet's eyes, quite perfect in every sense and she had a lot to learn from her. Their friendship was the most valuable thing in the world. For Emma, Harriet's company was very welcome, now that she didn't have Mrs Weston at her beck and call. As suspected, Harriet was naïve and knew very little of the world, never questioning whatever one might tell her, but she was so kind, grateful and engaging that Emma liked her more and more each day.

During their walks, Harriet had revealed that she was friends with a family called the Martins, who were farmers, and often talked of how generous they were and how much she enjoyed visiting them. At first, Emma had been amused by Harriet's exclamations of how nice the small house was and how well-kept all the darling little animals were, but it had come to her attention that the unmarried son, Robert, had been mentioned a little *too* often.

She was sure that the Martins were nice sort of people, but really, Harriet could not possibly be entertaining the idea of *liking* Mr Martin? A farmer! It would not do. No matter how kind-hearted they might be, farmers were so far beneath Emma's social status that she could not bear the idea of her

EMMA

dear, sweet friend associating with ill-mannered, unpolished farm workers, who apparently spent their time giving away cows to impressionable young ladies. She must guide her friend away from such danger.

This was exactly why Harriet needed Emma in her life.

'Did I tell you that Mr Martin once walked three miles to fetch me walnuts, just because I had said that I liked them?' Harriet said brightly.

'Indeed! Walnuts *and* a cow, what more could you possibly want?' Emma cleared her throat, determined to get to the bottom of this. 'Tell me more about Mr Martin, Harriet. I suppose, being a farmer, he does not read?'

'Oh, yes he does! I recommended him a book I enjoyed, *Romance of the Forest*,' Harriet enthused. 'He is very good at cards, too. He won very often and then I believe he started to let me win, because I didn't really understand any of the rules and yet suddenly I had quite a streak.'

'And what does he look like? Is he handsome?'

'I thought him plain at first. Although' – she hesitated, smiling slightly – 'I think him less plain now that I've spent time with him.'

It was worse than Emma thought. Something must be done and quickly.

A man appeared ahead of them on the path coming the other way. He stopped on seeing them and then broke into a wide smile, making his way towards them with some urgency.

'It's Mr Martin!' Harriet gasped, her hands flying to her bonnet to check the ribbon was still in a neat bow.

Emma studied Mr Martin as he approached and

was surprised to see that he was better presented than she had imagined, but other than that, she could not see any advantage.

After introductions were made, Emma walked slightly ahead and let them talk for a few minutes, listening carefully to their exchange, before Harriet excused herself from his company as Miss Woodhouse must not be kept waiting.

'How funny we should bump into him!' Harriet exclaimed in a flutter. 'I am sure my curls are all out of place from the breeze today. I hope he did not notice. What did you think of him, Miss Woodhouse?'

'He is very plain, just as you said,' Emma replied calmly, hoping she might inspire some composure in her flustered friend. 'But what surprised me was that I had not expected him to be quite so clownish! So far from what a gentleman should be.'

Harriet faltered, blinking up at Emma in a mixture of confusion and embarrassment.

'To be sure,' she began carefully, her cheeks growing pinker, 'he is not as … refined as many gentlemen of your acquaintance but—'

'I pity the woman he marries,' Emma sighed, smoothing a crease in her shawl. 'With no education and no manners, he is sure to age into quite an oaf! He is already awkward, for I daresay he could not meet my eye on introduction, and he is thoughtless, too. If he is like that now, what shall he be in a few years? It is not to be thought of!'

'That will be very bad. Very bad indeed,' Harriet said solemnly. 'But Miss Woodhouse, he is not thoughtless. Do not you remember the walnut story?'

'If you say so, dear. I just thought it odd he did not think to read that book you so kindly recommended him,' Emma said, glancing sympathetically at Harriet. 'I overheard him tell you just now he forgot. To me, it seems a grave offence to forget your book recommendation, as though your opinion is not important to him.'

'Yes.' Harriet frowned. 'I wonder he did not remember the book.'

They walked on in silence for a few minutes as Emma left Harriet to ponder her comments, noting her friend's pleasingly vexed expression.

'Mr Elton is so obliging and well-mannered,' Emma said suddenly, causing Harriet to look up. 'He is so kind, don't you think? What's more, he is handsome and has a satisfactory income. Now, he is what I call a *gentleman*.'

'Yes,' Harriet agreed, nodding slowly. 'Mr Elton is very genteel.'

'Many have commented on Mr Elton's change of late; he seems even more cheerful than usual. I have thought on it and realised this change came about just after he met you, Harriet.'

'Oh!' Harriet blushed, smiling bashfully. 'I am sure he cannot have noticed me.'

Emma looked surprised. 'Didn't I tell you the

very kind thing he said about you? It was so lovely;
I could not get it out of my head all day.'

'Mr Elton spoke of *me*? Whatever for!'

Emma smiled, stopping to take Harriet's hands
in hers and look at her with a mischievous twinkle
in her eyes.

'If you insist, I shall tell you what he said,' she
whispered as Harriet giggled excitedly. 'And then
let us talk of nothing else all the way home!'

CHAPTER FOUR

The painting was Emma's idea.

She had been musing over the notion of painting a portrait of Harriet for some days, but waited until Mr Elton paid a visit to Hartfield one morning to make the suggestion out loud.

'It would be a delight!' cried Mr Elton with such feeling that Emma could not help but smile. 'What a charming subject for your exceptional talent!'

'Please, Mr Elton, you exaggerate my skill,' Emma insisted. 'But I should like to take up my brush again and Harriet is so beautiful, her features so delicate.'

'And such improvement in her manner since

her introduction to you Miss Woodhouse,' Mr Elton affirmed warmly. 'Thanks to your encouragement, she is very graceful now and more at ease in conversation.'

'I have done very little. Oh, how I should like to capture her grace you speak of in a picture. What a shame!'

'A shame, Miss Woodhouse? Why so?'

'Because she would not sit for me,' Emma explained with a hopeless sigh. 'She is too modest. I suppose I could ask her, but I know very well that she will think I am only being a generous friend when I speak of her qualities. As such, she will likely not be persuaded. If only the idea could come from someone else!'

Mr Elton became pensive at Emma's downcast expression and then his eyes lit up as an answer presented itself out of the blue.

'What if I should persuade her? I do not know her so well. Perhaps she would be more inclined to listen to my praise than yours!'

'Mr Elton,' Emma gasped, pressing a hand against her heart, 'I had not thought of that. An excellent idea! Here she comes now; let us see what we can do.'

As Harriet approached from the other side of the drawing room, Mr Elton posed the question of a portrait to her at once and, when she hesitated with her answer, he convinced her that it would give the present company great pleasure should she sit for Miss Woodhouse.

Startled at his earnest pressing, Harriet found herself agreeing to it.

'I cannot thank you enough, Harriet, for I have missed painting,' Emma admitted. 'Some time ago I attempted a portrait of my sister's husband, Mr John Knightley. It was close to being finished when Isabella declared it did not do her husband justice. After all that work! That was it; I vowed never to paint again. But as there are no husbands and wives here at the moment, I am delighted, Harriet, to break my vow for you.'

'As you say, Miss Woodhouse,' Mr Elton repeated in a serious tone, 'no husbands and wives here *at the moment.*'

Emma and Harriet could barely contain themselves as Mr Elton bowed his head and moved away to join Mr Knightley, who was presently in conversation with Mr Woodhouse about the dangers of broccoli.

'My dear Miss Woodhouse, what do you think he meant?' Harriet asked breathlessly, watching him go.

'I think we can both guess what he meant,' Emma replied. 'We had better start the painting straight away; I would not want to keep your admirer waiting!'

Within a few minutes, Emma had decided on the size of the portrait and that she would be painting it in watercolour. As she directed Harriet to position herself in a good spot of natural light by the window, Mr Elton excused himself from Mr Woodhouse and Mr Knightley's company so that he might closely observe the first sitting. Emma could hardly believe how well her plan was falling into place. That he should fall in love with Harriet was never doubted, but to make his feelings for her so apparent so quickly was unexpected. How little Emma had to do for this excellent match!

'Mr Elton, if you insist on observing, pray do sit down,' Emma suggested, preparing her brush as he paced about impatiently behind her chair. 'This will take some time.'

'Sit, Miss Woodhouse!' Mr Elton shook his head. 'How can one sit at such an occasion? I do not have the patience. No, no, I am happy to stand. Stand and admire.'

Harriet blushed to her roots as Emma gave her a knowing look.

The first sitting went very well. Harriet was

patient and the lighting and setting was all to Emma's liking. The only problem was Mr Elton's fidgeting. He could not stand still and constantly asked if he

could peer over Emma's shoulder and see how the painting was coming on. Emma appreciated his enthusiasm, but it was a tad off-putting.

When he requested to join them again the next day for the second and final sitting, Emma was tempted to say no, so that she could paint in peace, but his adoration for Harriet was so pleasing, she couldn't possibly turn him down.

'You have made her too tall,' Mr Knightley observed when the painting was finished and unveiled to those at Hartfield after dinner the following evening.

'I have not,' Emma protested, although she knew she had.

'Not too tall at all,' Mr Elton jumped in. 'Consider, Mr Knightley, Miss Smith is sitting down in the portrait, so ... well ... it's all to do with the proportions, you know. It gives the *idea* of Miss Smith's height perfectly.'

Emma was not sure he was making sense but, as it was a staunch defence in the face of Mr Knightley's criticism, she nodded along in agreement anyway.

'It is very pretty. No one draws like you, Emma!'

her father declared. 'But she will catch cold.'

'Who will catch cold, Papa?'

'Miss Smith!'

'I am very warm at present, Mr Woodhouse,' Harriet assured him.

'But she will catch cold here in the portrait,' he explained, holding it up for them all to see. 'She is painted sitting outside with just a little shawl!'

'Oh, Papa.' Emma laughed, gesturing to the blue skies at the top of the canvas. 'It is supposed to be a warm summer's day. Look at the sunshine on the tree next to her.'

'But what if a cool breeze should sweep in? She would then be in great danger. It would be much better if she was not sitting outdoors.'

'Ah, Mr Woodhouse, I see what you are saying,' Mr Elton said hurriedly, 'but I must say that I think it very happy that she is outdoors! Why, look at that tree! It has such ... spirit! She looks so very well next to that tree. This painting is admirable! I can't stop looking at it!'

Harriet bowed her head modestly, smiling so much that her jaw began to ache.

'Well, there is only one thing to do. We must take it to London and get it framed,' Mr Woodhouse concluded.

'Perhaps Isabella could help us with that,' Emma suggested.

Mr Woodhouse gasped. 'My dear child! I cannot allow my daughter to be gallivanting about London in the winter, searching for a frame! It might snow!'

'But she lives in London, Papa,' Emma said. 'I'm sure it would not be any trouble.'

'Might I be entrusted with such an important task?' Mr Elton suddenly said in a gallant voice. 'I can ride to London and see to it that this masterpiece is adorned with the perfect frame.'

'Mr Elton, do not be absurd!' Emma cried, stealing a look at Harriet, whose eyes were upon him, wide with adoration. 'It would be much too troublesome—'

'Miss Woodhouse, let me insist! To play some part in the framing of Miss Smith's portrait would give me more pleasure than I deserve.'

'It is decided then,' Mr Woodhouse said, pleased to get it sorted so that he might be able to go and sit in his chair for a doze. He passed Mr Elton the painting. 'Thank you, sir.'

'What a precious piece,' Mr Elton said with a tender sigh, taking the picture in his hands and gazing upon the subject.

Emma turned to look at Mr Knightley in triumph when she saw that he was attempting to hide an amused smile. She frowned at him with great disapproval. Yes, she had to admit that Mr Elton's displays of admiration were a little over the top, but Mr Knightley had no right to find them so funny.

Still, it didn't matter what Mr Knightley thought. Mr Elton and Harriet would have the last laugh.

Emma wouldn't be surprised if a proposal was made by the end of the month.

CHAPTER FIVE

'He proposed!'

Emma gasped at Harriet's announcement. Mr Elton had only left for London that morning and here was Harriet at Hartfield, clutching a letter which Emma could see had Harriet's name penned across the front in very elegant handwriting.

'He proposed!' Emma repeated, ushering her friend towards her so they could sit down together. 'And so soon! He must be very much in love with you, Harriet, to acknowledge his feelings so quickly!'

'Oh, Miss Woodhouse!' Harriet cried. 'Isn't it extraordinary? As you know, I was here with you all day and then I returned for dinner and Mrs Goddard told me he had called just an hour before. And he'd left this letter just sitting on—'

'But how could Mr Elton have paid a visit this afternoon?' Emma asked.

'Mr Elton?' Harriet looked at her in confusion. 'Why are you talking of Mr Elton?'

'But . . .' Emma glanced down at the letter in Harriet's hand.

'Oh, you think the proposal is from Mr Elton!' Harriet shook her head. 'No, Miss Woodhouse. It is from Mr Martin! Mr Robert Martin! You met him once when we were out walking, do you recall? He was the one who gave me that cow!'

Harriet had mistaken Emma's baffled expression for forgetfulness.

'Mr Martin proposed to you,' Emma said slowly, drawing back in disappointment.

'Yes! Oh, Miss Woodhouse, what shall I do? I came here straight away. Will you read the letter?' She handed it over eagerly. 'Pray do!'

Emma opened the letter and began to read, watched carefully by Harriet.

'What do you think? Is it too short? Too long? Is it a good letter?' she asked desperately.

'It is a good letter. No grammatical errors and a good length too. He writes sincerely and with great warmth.' Emma passed the letter back. 'One of his sisters must have helped him.'

'Well?' Harriet asked, clutching the now very crumpled letter.

'Well, what?'

'What do I do?' she cried, so agitated she could

hardly sit still.

'What do you mean? You must answer it, of course!'

'But what shall I say? Miss Woodhouse, do tell me what to write!'

'Harriet.' Emma smiled. 'I cannot tell you what to write! This letter has to be all your own. You give your answer plainly, without any doubts or hesitations, and that is that! You don't need to worry yourself about disappointing him. I am sure he will get over it.'

'Oh.' Harriet paused. 'You think I should refuse him, then?'

'My dear Harriet, what ever can you mean? You don't mean to accept him?' Emma stared at her. 'Ah, I have made a mistake. I assumed ... Well, I thought you were asking my advice on how to *word* your answer. Not on what your answer should be.'

They sat in silence. Harriet bit her lip nervously. Emma watched her and realised that Harriet was in very real danger of falling into an attachment beneath her station in society. Her dear, dear friend marry a farmer such as *Mr Martin*? She could not allow it. She must carefully nudge her in the right direction.

Although it pained her to be reserved with Harriet, Emma withdrew her hand from where it had been comfortingly placed on Harriet's wrist.

'You mean to accept his proposal, then,' Emma said coldly.

Her manner instantly sparked panic in Harriet, who looked up in anguish.

'No! I mean ... well ... oh, I need you to tell me what to do, Miss Woodhouse!'

'I cannot, Harriet. This must be your decision.'

Harriet sighed, contemplating the letter. 'I did not know that he liked me so much.'

Emma pursed her lips and waited. When more silence followed, Emma thought it best to offer some kind of guidance so they were not sitting here for the rest of the century.

'I believe that if a woman has any doubts about a marriage proposal, then she should not accept it,' Emma stated. 'One must never enter marriage with half a heart.'

Harriet nodded slowly. 'That is true.'

'Then' – Emma leaned forwards and grasped both of Harriet's hands in hers, so that she may look directly into her eyes – 'if you prefer Mr Martin to any other man you have ever met, if you think him the most agreeable man, superior to any other gentleman, why should you hesitate?'

Harriet let out a long sigh. She rose to her feet and paced across the room to stand by the fire. Suddenly, she turned to face Emma.

'As you cannot help me in this matter, I must do the best I can myself. And I have made a decision. I think. I have very much ... *almost* made up my mind.'

'Very well,' Emma said, straightening in

anticipation. 'And your answer?'

'I am determined ... uh ... I will ... I am determined to ... refuse Mr Martin,' Harriet said, before rushing over to sit back down. 'Do you think I am right?'

Emma breathed a sigh of relief and smiled warmly at her friend.

'Now that you have come to your own decision, I can safely tell you my opinion without fear of influencing you. Harriet, you are perfectly right to refuse him. I could not tell you my own selfish reason before, but now I am free to say how sorry I would have been to lose you! If you married Mr Martin, I would not have been able to visit you. It would have grieved me to lose your acquaintance.'

Emma's words struck Harriet with great force. She had not even thought of that! If she had accepted him, she might have been thrown out of all good society! And she had only just joined it!

'Dear me, Miss Woodhouse, I could never risk

losing your friendship! You have been so kind to me.'

'Harriet,' Emma said, her heart filled with warmth, 'I could not have been parted from you. And to think it may have been so, just because you liked a cow! Now, it is time to answer him.'

Though Emma insisted the response should be all Harriet's doing, she dictated every sentence, and soon it was finished, sealed and sent. Harriet felt terrible that she should be causing pain to such a kind man and, seeing Harriet's sorrow, it was left to Emma to remind her of a more suitable prospect.

'I wonder where Mr Elton is right now,' Emma mused out loud. 'Adoring your portrait no doubt. Showing it off in London to his friends and family there.'

Harriet smiled softly and Emma was encouraged to go on.

'I mentioned to him your collection of riddles that you told me about the other day. He was very interested and said how charming it was for you to keep a book of them. In fact, he expressed a wish to contribute a riddle to your book.'

'Did he?' Harriet asked curiously. 'That would be very kind of him. I suppose he is very clever.' She hesitated. 'Do you really think he is showing my portrait to his family in London?'

'And telling them that its subject is all the more

beautiful in person.'

Emma was satisfied to see Harriet smiling shyly at the idea and the rest of their time together was spent imagining Mr Elton's current conversations and endeavours.

And though Harriet's mind often wandered to poor Mr Martin, picturing his face as he read her refusal, she hoped that, as Miss Woodhouse assured her, in time she would forget him.

CHAPTER SIX

'All right,' Mr Knightley sighed. 'I'll admit it, Emma. You have improved Miss Smith. She seems to have grown up under your instruction.'

Emma was pleased, knowing that Mr Knightley would never willingly compliment her unless he truly meant it. Harriet was at Mrs Goddard's for the day and Mr Woodhouse was outside for his daily walk in the garden, so Mr Knightley could speak freely.

'Thank you, Mr Knightley,' Emma replied graciously.

'I have reason to believe that your friend, Miss Smith, is soon to receive an offer of marriage,'

Mr Knightley said, smiling. 'Someone has confided in me that he is deeply in love with her.'

Emma's eyes widened. 'Who makes you his confidant?'

'Robert Martin. She stayed with his family over the summer.'

'Oh.' Emma could not hide her disappointment. She knew that Mr Elton looked up to Mr Knightley, as almost everybody in the village did, and thought he might have spoken to Mr Knightley of his feelings for Harriet. Mr Knightley was too happy to tell of Robert Martin's intentions to notice Emma's reaction, however, and he continued.

'He came to see me two evenings ago wanting my advice on the matter. He told me how much he loved her, how he could think of nothing but marrying her, and wanted to know whether I thought she was too young. He also worried that now she was spending so much time here at Hartfield, she might think herself too high in society for him, but I told him that was nonsense.' He paused thoughtfully. 'I never hear better sense from anyone than Robert Martin. He is quite one of the best men I know. Harriet Smith is a lucky woman.'

Emma smiled to herself at Mr Knightley's assumption.

'In return for you telling me so, let me tell you what I know. Mr Martin proposed to Harriet yesterday. He was refused.'

Mr Knightley stared at her in confusion.

'I beg your pardon?'

'He proposed to her yesterday and he was refused,' Emma repeated.

'I'm not sure I understand.'

'Mr Knightley,' Emma laughed, 'I'm not sure I can put it more plainly. What confuses you? He wrote to her with an offer of marriage and she wrote back refusing him.'

Mr Knightley was so shocked and angry that he grew quite red in the face and got to his feet in order to pace about the room. Emma watched him in amusement.

'Then Harriet Smith is a bigger fool than I thought,' he said crossly.

Emma sighed, rolling her eyes. 'Of course, no man can understand why a woman could possibly want to turn down an offer of marriage.'

'Emma, don't talk nonsense,' he snapped, surprising her with his tone. 'Mr Martin is an excellent match for Harriet and it was understood that she had feelings for him. I very much hope you are mistaken in this.'

'I am not mistaken. I saw her answer.'

'Saw it?' Mr Knightley stopped pacing to look at her sternly. 'You *wrote* her answer. Oh, Emma, what have you done?'

'If I had written it, which I am not admitting to, but if I had, it would have been the right thing to do. Mr Martin is not her equal. Just because he has given her a *cow* that does not give him grounds to think he can marry her.'

'No, he is not her equal! He is her superior in every way! Your infatuation with Harriet Smith blinds you! No one knows who her parents are or what her fortune may be, and, yes, she is pretty, I grant you, but she is ignorant and silly where he is intelligent and wise.' Mr Knightley paused before

adding, 'I admit, I'm not sure what you mean when you speak of a cow.'

'I could not see my dear friend married to someone so beneath me in social status! It would be intolerable! Why should she accept the first offer of marriage she receives? She is only beginning to be known to good society.'

'Emma, I know what you are thinking, believing yourself to be a matchmaker,' Mr Knightley growled, barely able to keep his countenance. 'Mr Elton will not marry Harriet Smith. He sees himself a respectable man and is unlikely to make a reckless decision when it comes to marriage. He intends to marry well. I have often heard him speak of some wealthy ladies in Bath, whose situation and fortune sparked his interest.'

Emma's eyes fell to her lap. His words affected her and she had a moment of doubt as to her actions, but then felt comforted that Mr Knightley had not witnessed Mr Elton around Harriet as she had.

'Mr Knightley, we had better not discuss the matter further as we will only quarrel.'

'I could not agree more,' he said and with a quick bow of his head, he stormed out of the room and left the house, muttering to himself. He knew how much Mr Martin loved Harriet Smith and felt keenly disappointed on his behalf.

Emma could not sit a moment longer, too agitated by Mr Knightley's manner of speaking to her. Apart from her father, Mr Knightley's opinion of her mattered the most of all her acquaintances. That he should be so displeased with her was greatly vexing, even if she knew she was right.

She remained in a troubled state for the rest of the day and was only cheered at Mr Elton's return from London and his popping by to drop a note at Hartfield, a riddle for Harriet's collection. When Harriet arrived later, Emma opened it eagerly and they read it together.

My first displays the wealth and pomp of kings,
Lords of the earth! Their luxury and ease.
Another view of man, my second brings,
Behold him there, the monarch of the seas!

Emma got its meaning at once and waited as Harriet read it again and again and again before she cried out in exasperation. 'Oh, Miss Woodhouse! I cannot understand it!'

'Let me help you,' Emma said kindly, pointing to the first bit. 'These first two lines – where are the "displays of wealth and pomp" shown, dear?'

Harriet looked thoughtful. 'Um. Wealth and pomp. Pomp and wealth. Oh dear. Wealth and pomp. Oh, I shall never know the answer to this riddle!'

'In court!'

'Of course!' Harried exclaimed. 'Wealth and pomp of kings in court!'

'So, we have *court*,' Emma said. 'And the second

bit, what do you think "monarch of the seas" could be?'

'Monarch of the seas,' Harriet said slowly, her forehead furrowed in deep concentration. 'Mermaid? Oh dear, Court Mermaid makes no sense!'

'Ship!' Emma laughed. 'He means *ship*. So, we can put those together and we have the meaning of the riddle!'

'Ship! And court. Court and ship.' Harriet suddenly gasped. 'He writes of *courtship*!'

'Oh, Harriet,' Emma sighed, 'Mr Elton has written you a riddle about courtship.'

Harriet was left in a flutter of happiness and spent the next hour reading the four lines repeatedly, every now and then letting out utterances of 'oh' and 'heavens'.

Emma's mood was duly lifted and she only wished Mr Knightley had been there to witness this clear admission of Mr Elton's intentions.

CHAPTER SEVEN

'Why are you not married, Miss Woodhouse?' Harriet asked on one of their walks.

They had just paid a visit to a sick and poor family a little way out from Highbury. Emma tried as best she could to often visit those with so little and bring them food, for she knew how lucky her situation in life was.

'Because, Harriet, I have very little intention of ever marrying,' Emma replied, looking out across the fields.

Harriet was stunned. 'I cannot believe you!'

Emma laughed at her friend's expression. 'Can you not? Think on it, Harriet, why should I want to marry? I do not need money or situation, and when a woman marries, her property and inheritance becomes her husband's. I am perfectly happy to be in charge of mine. And I know very well that I shall never be so important in anyone's eyes than in my father's.' Emma paused before adding, 'It would be different I am sure, were I to fall in love, but I never have and I don't think I ever shall.'

Harriet pondered her friend's answer before shaking her head. 'But to end up an old maid like Miss Bates. It would be terribly sad.'

'I should never be like Miss Bates! She is ridiculous, for a start, and never stops talking. One can only feel sympathy for unmarried old maids who are poor. I am not poor. A single woman of good fortune is always respectable,' Emma concluded.

'But what will you *do* when you're old if you are not married?' Harriet asked, still trying to get her head round the idea.

'I will read and draw, and have a wonderful time with all my dear nephews and nieces!' Emma smiled, thinking on them. 'Isabella and John's children are all I will need to keep me happy. A niece can dote on me as I grow old.'

'Has Miss Bates spoken to you of her niece, Jane Fairfax?' Harriet suddenly asked. 'I hear she is very accomplished.'

Emma pursed her lips. She had heard so often of Jane Fairfax as to be terribly tired of her. Jane Fairfax, who had grown up in the care of wealthy guardians, was Miss Bates's favourite topic. Emma had met Jane several times, but she could not find much reason to like her.

'Yes, to be sure, Jane Fairfax is accomplished in *some* people's eyes,' Emma said haughtily. 'Although I do wish she would write to her aunt less. Her letters are read aloud to me forty times. I wish her well but she tires me to death.'

Emma came to a sudden stop on the lane,

grabbing her friend's arm and gesturing to the house before them. 'Look, Harriet, that is Mr Elton's house.'

Harriet gazed up at it in admiration. 'How sweet it is! I like those yellow curtains.'

Continuing their walk down the lane at a slower

pace so that Harriet could cast lingering looks back at the vicarage, they turned a bend and saw a gentleman approaching, none other than Mr Elton himself.

'Mr Elton!' Emma said, greeting him warmly. He could not have looked more pleased to find himself in their company.

'Miss Woodhouse, Miss Smith,' he said, bowing his head. 'Are you on your way home?'

'Yes, Miss Smith has just made a charitable visit to that poor, sick woman down the way,' Emma said, making eyes at Harriet, who looked confused. 'If only I had the goodness of Harriet's heart!'

Mr Elton only smiled. 'May I walk you both home?'

'That is very kind of you,' Emma said, as he fell into step with them. She was careful to manoeuvre herself so that he was next to Harriet. He struck up conversation, asking after Mr Woodhouse and Emma gave a short answer, her mind too occupied by working out how she may leave them alone together for a moment. An idea came to her.

'Oh dear!' she cried, stooping to the ground and arranging her dress so that her boot was covered. 'My lace has broken. Pray, be kind enough to go ahead and let me catch you up in just a minute.'

Mr Elton faltered, unsure of what a gentleman should do in the case of a broken boot lace, but Emma insisted so heavily that he eventually walked on with Harriet. When she was sure they were not looking back, Emma broke off the lace and threw it in the ditch, for it would not do to be caught lying when she re-joined them.

After an appropriate amount of time, she walked on slowly. She was very pleased with herself for offering Mr Elton a perfect proposal opportunity. He had Harriet alone to himself without it being improper, and to ask for her hand in marriage on the pretty country lane just a little way from his house was particularly romantic.

Turning a corner, Emma realised that they had stopped and were waiting for her. Wondering if that meant the deed had already been done, she approached apprehensively, catching their conversation.

'Oh yes,' Mr Elton was saying cheerily, 'I had Stilton cheese, celery and beetroot! Miss Woodhouse, there you are. I was just telling Miss Smith about my dinner yesterday.'

'Ah,' Emma said, 'how ... charming.'

She was a little put out by his missing a chance

such as this one. What a waste of a good proposal spot! And a good boot lace!

But as they walked on, Emma reminded herself that a marriage proposal was not something a sensible gentleman would do on a whim. No, Mr Elton, she was sure, would want to plan it carefully.

Reluctantly, Emma admitted that she would have to leave the proposal itself to Mr Elton. All she could do now was wait.

CHAPTER EIGHT

While Emma did not wish to apologise to Mr Knightley for their argument as she had been right all along, she did want to make up with him.

They had not seen each other since their heated discussion regarding Mr Martin's proposal several days ago, and Emma found herself missing his daily visits. She hoped that he was simply very busy and that he was not avoiding Hartfield on purpose. Either way, she felt it was about time to clear the air.

The perfect chance arose when her sister Isabella and Mr John Knightley arrived at Hartfield with their five children for Christmas. It was only right that Emma invited Mr Knightley to dine with them on the evening of their arrival and so she sent out the formal invitation promptly.

'Dear me,' Mr Woodhouse proclaimed, a little overwhelmed as three of the Knightley children began to run rings round his chair, 'so many children, Isabella! How do you keep track of them all? You must fall ill very often with so much to do!'

'I have wonderful nursery-maids, Papa. And the children are all very good so they do not cause much trouble,' Isabella said affectionately as one of the children gave his brother a good pinch while she was looking the other way.

The youngest of Isabella's children, a little girl of eight months named after her aunt, was asleep in Emma's arms. Emma was determined to hold on to her until Mr Knightley was there. She had plotted that if there was a baby with such delightfully chubby cheeks present, Mr Knightley could not possibly be grouchy with her. Her plan worked.

Mr Knightley arrived and soon drifted over to where Emma sat, a smile on his face as he looked down on the sleeping child.

'Little Emma. She is beautiful,' he remarked, admiring her.

'Yes,' Emma replied gently. 'There. At least we agree on *something*.'

Mr Knightley lifted his eyes to meet hers and she could see that his expression bore no ill will, but instead was teasing.

'I have missed our disagreements,' he said.

'I am not surprised that *you* have missed them,' Emma sighed, her spirits lifting, 'as they always arise from me somehow being in the wrong.'

'Naturally,' he agreed, 'but then I am older than you. It makes sense that I am wiser and have the advantage of experience.'

'Perhaps that was so when I was young, but I am now twenty-one and catching up with you in knowledge.'

'Is that so?' Mr Knightley looked back to the baby. 'Little Emma, tell your aunt that she is still to learn to stop bringing up old arguments when the tempers have passed.'

'Little Emma is far more intelligent than I am

and knows better than to listen to you,' Emma said, making him chuckle. 'Mr Knightley, I will leave it alone but let me say that, though we argued, we both had good intentions for our friends. I hope Mr Martin was not too disappointed.'

'No man could have been more so.'

'I am very sorry for him,' she said, before moving baby Emma slightly so she could hold out her hand. 'Shake hands with me, dear friend, and let us forget and move on.'

Mr Knightley took her hand and kissed it lightly. 'Very well.'

'Come, come, Emma!' Isabella said, gesturing for them to move closer to the fire and holding her arms out to cradle baby Emma. 'Tell me all the news of Highbury. How is the new Mrs Weston?'

'Poor Miss Taylor!' cried out Mr Woodhouse. 'We do not see her as often as we would like.'

'Dear Papa, we see them almost every day,' Emma corrected him, laughing. 'They are very happy together, Isabella.'

'I am pleased to hear it,' Isabella said. 'Has Frank Churchill come to visit them?'

'Not yet,' Emma said. 'But I am sure he will come.'

'In his own time,' Mr Knightley muttered under his breath.

Emma smiled to Isabella, telling her, 'Mr Knightley cannot bear the idea of a man who will not do his duty. But there will surely be a good reason why he has not come.'

'And Mrs Bates? Miss Bates?' Isabella continued with her enquiries.

'Mrs Bates had a terrible cold about a month ago,' Mr Woodhouse informed her gravely. 'Mr Perry, the village apothecary, tells me that colds have not been as prominent this winter in the village as last year, which is pleasing. A very clever man, Mr Perry.'

'And how is Miss Bates's dear, sweet niece, Jane Fairfax?'

It was all Emma could do not to roll her eyes at the question. She could not understand the world's obsession with dull Jane Fairfax.

'I hear she is well,' was all Emma could think of to say.

'It has been so long since I have seen her now that I live in London,' Isabella noted. 'She is such an accomplished, elegant girl and she must bring great happiness to her aunt when she comes to visit. It is a shame she does not live in Highbury, for she is your age, is she not, Emma? She would make a charming companion for you.'

Emma felt a laugh rising in her throat and had to pretend to have a coughing fit to cover it up. Mr Knightley gave her a sly look.

'Yes, it is a shame she is not here more often,' he said breezily, as one of the children ran round to give Emma a helpful thump on her back.

'Thank you, dear,' she said to her nephew, before coming back to the conversation. 'Yes, well, I have a charming companion already in Harriet Smith. I look forward to you meeting her, Isabella.'

'Will she be at the Westons' Christmas Eve dinner party?'

'She will indeed,' Emma said cheerfully, thinking of Mr Elton being in attendance also. 'It may be a *very* significant event for her.'

The only one to catch her meaning, Mr Knightley sighed and shook his head, but she would not stop smiling.

'The Westons' Christmas Eve party will be a significant event indeed,' Mr Woodhouse declared. 'For, despite the bitter cold, I will be leaving the house for it!'

CHAPTER NINE

On the morning of Christmas Eve, Emma Woodhouse was given some news of the most dreadful kind: Miss Harriet Smith had a sore throat.

That so delicate a creature as Miss Smith could be struck by such an illness was distressing enough to all who heard of it, but that she should have to miss out on the Westons' Christmas party seemed to be injustice of the cruellest nature!

Emma had felt sure that Mr Elton would be so affected by the news that he might skip the party altogether, but he seemed in cheerful spirits and she found herself admiring his ability to keep a joyful demeanour at a time that was no doubt grievous for him.

Emma did notice, however, that Mr Elton remained rather close by her at the party in the lead up to dinner. At first, she thought his constant lingering and persistent questions after her health might be down to his wondering how to bring Harriet's health easily into conversation. But then ...

'Miss Woodhouse, I must implore you to stop visiting Miss Smith.'

'Mr Elton, whatever do you—'

'You put yourself at risk! What if you should catch a sore throat, too? What then?' He shook his head in horror. 'No, it will not do. Are you quite warm enough there? Would you like to move closer to the fire?'

Emma was so alarmed by his strange behaviour that she was very pleased to find she was not seated next to him at dinner, and was next to Mr Weston. Even so, as Mr Weston went on about his recent letter from Frank Churchill, who promised to visit in two weeks, Emma still felt Mr Elton's gaze upon her.

When the ladies retired to the drawing room after dinner, Emma took her place next to Mrs Weston and Isabella on the sofa and they spoke of Frank Churchill's impending visit.

'I do hope his aunt will release him and allow him to visit us.' Mrs Weston sighed. 'I wonder that she will ever let him come.'

'Everyone knows of Mrs Churchill.' Isabella grimaced. 'She is not a woman to be trifled with. Poor Frank Churchill, I'm afraid he must obey her every whim!'

'He will come soon, I am sure.' Emma smiled at Mrs Weston encouragingly. 'Let us stay hopeful and not let Mrs Churchill and her foul temper dampen our festive spirits.'

After a time, the men joined the ladies in the drawing room and Mr Elton entered the room very jolly indeed, sitting himself between Mrs Weston and Emma so decidedly that the ladies had no time to move apart so that he may fit in.

'Miss Woodhouse, your father wishes to go home,' Mr Elton said, turning his back to Mrs Weston, who was trying very subtly to pull her gown out from underneath his bottom. 'Mr Knightley has called the carriages for us.'

As Emma reluctantly said goodbye to Mr and Mrs Weston, her father, Isabella and John left and stepped into the first carriage, which departed for Hartfield. Emma therefore found herself in the second carriage with Mr Elton, who had been offered a lift home by Mr Woodhouse.

'It is starting to snow.' Emma smiled, looking out the window of the carriage as it set off. 'How pretty it is and I daresay—'

'Miss Woodhouse!' Mr Elton suddenly cried with such passion that Emma slammed back in her seat. 'I must tell you how I love you!'

'Good heavens! Mr Elton, what—'

'I have longed to tell you how I love you! And that I wish to marry you! I must take this opportunity of being alone with you to reveal it all! If you refuse me, I am ready to die!'

'Mr Elton! Please!' Emma held her hand up to him. 'Sir, you forget yourself. You have become confused! You are talking to *me*, Miss Woodhouse. I shall deliver your message to Miss Smith, but no more of this to me.'

'Miss Smith?' Mr Elton wrinkled his nose. 'What message would I want to send to *Miss Smith*?'

Emma stared at him. 'I cannot understand your behaviour, Mr Elton, and I can only explain it to be in some way down to the party muddling your spirits. You are not yourself at present. I am very happy to forget all about this and will not mention it to Miss Smith. Please do calm yourself at once.'

'I am not muddled in the least,' Mr Elton said, with an alarmingly dreamy look in his eyes as he gazed at her across the carriage. 'My meaning could not be more clear. I wonder why you should speak of Miss Smith at a moment such as this one!'

Before Emma could stop him, he got up and positioned himself on her side of the carriage, leaning in rather close.

'I am in love with you, Miss Woodhouse, and I hope you will answer my proposal of marriage favourably.'

Emma could see that he was perfectly serious and not confused in the least.

'Mr Elton, please! I am astonished! I cannot understand after your behaviour the last few months and the attentions you have paid to Miss Smith that you would be interested in proposing to me!'

'Good God!' Mr Elton cried, amused. 'I have never thought of Miss Smith! Only that she was your friend, but other than that I couldn't care if she was alive or dead! Who could think of Miss Smith when Miss Woodhouse is near? I am sure you have noticed my attentions to you. You have encouraged them!'

'Encouraged them! No, sir, I only encouraged them in that I believed them directed to Miss Smith. You wrote her the riddle of courtship!'

'I was sure to leave that at your home. It was for you.'

'You insisted on taking her portrait to London!'

'I insisted on taking the portrait *you* had painted to London.'

Emma closed her eyes in despair. 'Mr Elton, am I to believe that you have never thought seriously of Miss Smith?'

'Never!' He snorted in a most disagreeable manner. 'Miss Smith! Look, she is a very good sort of girl and I wish her well, but I, Mr Elton, marry *Miss Smith*? I should like to think I am not so very desperate.' He hesitated as Emma looked at him in disgust. 'My visits to Hartfield have been for you only, and I have come to hope, through your many invitations, that my love for you is reciprocated.'

Emma took a deep breath and turned to look him straight in the eye.

'Mr Elton, I have seen you only as the admirer of my friend. I am exceedingly sorry for my mistake, but I do not see you in any other light than that of a friend. I must refuse your proposal. I have no intension of marrying.'

Mr Elton was so shocked at the rejection and then so angry, he could not utter another word. He moved back to the opposite side of the carriage and the two sat in tense, awkward silence for the rest of the journey. On reaching the vicarage, Mr Elton swung open the door and jumped out.

'Good night, Mr Elton,' Emma said as kindly as she could.

'Good night, Miss Woodhouse,' he replied coldly, slamming the carriage door shut behind him and storming into his house.

CHAPTER TEN

Oh dear. Oh dear, oh dear, oh dear!

Emma felt wretched. After the maid had curled her hair before bed, Emma sat at her dressing table, hardly believing what had happened. She felt so miserable and embarrassed by her misjudgement.

'I persuaded Harriet to like him,' she admitted to her reflection in the mirror. 'Poor, poor Harriet! She would not have even thought of him, had it not been for me!'

How could she have got it so wrong? She thought back on the past few months and remembered Mr Knightley's warning that Mr Elton would not marry below him. She recalled how eager Mr Elton was to compliment her painting, how attentive he was to her talents! She felt sick to her stomach. It was too mortifying.

And how little she thought of Mr Elton now. His addresses to her in the carriage had been too dramatic and arrogant to be founded in real love. Of that, Emma was quite certain. He had sought to marry well and set his eyes on Miss Woodhouse of Hartfield, an heiress of thirty thousand pounds. She could not feel sympathy for him; she believed that it would not be long before he proposed to an heiress elsewhere.

Well, this was a lesson well-learned for Emma. She would never attempt the art of matchmaking again. How badly she had played it this time. At least she was right in protecting Harriet from Mr Martin's advances. That she could allow herself to be congratulated on. *Well done, Emma!* But she had encouraged her dear friend's affections towards a most undeserving gentleman. If she had only given it more time and consideration, perhaps she would have found a better match.

William Cox, Emma thought. *He might do for Harriet. Although, he is a pert young lawyer and I'm not sure I could endure . . .*

Emma suddenly burst out laughing, blushing at her own relapse. Had she not just promised herself she would never attempt matchmaking again? Harriet had not even heard the news of Mr Elton yet and Emma was already busy finding her another suitor.

Poor Harriet! How Emma felt for her. She dreaded telling her friend of the news, but knew that it would have to be done and by her alone. She went to bed feeling miserable, every romantic hope for her friend shattered.

The weather was on Emma's side. It snowed so heavily over Christmas that all were confined to their houses and no visits could be paid in the village. Emma and Harriet could not see each other, nor could Mr Elton be expected to venture to Hartfield, so no suspicions were aroused in Emma's family when Mr Elton, having been such an attentive neighbour, was now strikingly absent.

Only Mr Knightley visited the family, acknowledging that no weather could keep him. Emma was grateful that she could have a few days to enjoy the company of her sister and the children without having to worry about her conversation with Harriet, but soon the snow stopped and the roads became clear again.

On the morning that Isabella and her family left for London, Mr Woodhouse received a letter from Mr Elton.

'He is to go to Bath for a few weeks to visit some friends there,' Mr Woodhouse read aloud to Emma, who was pleasantly surprised at the news. 'He had hoped to say goodbye in person, but was unable due to various circumstances of weather and business. Well!' Mr Woodhouse sighed, putting the letter down. 'I am alarmed by this. To take such a journey when it has only just stopped snowing! I hope he makes it to Bath safely, for the horses shall not like the cold snow on their hooves, to be sure! They might rally together in protest and run wild with the carriage in tow, or stomp on anyone who comes near!'

On hearing Mr Elton had gone away, Emma resolved to visit Harriet the very next day. She could not put it off any longer.

'Dear Harriet, I must tell you something,' she said, sitting down alone with her at Mrs Goddard's. 'Mr Elton has gone to Bath for a few weeks. He is to visit some friends there.'

'Oh,' Harriet said, picking up on Emma's grave tone. 'Is something wrong, Miss Woodhouse? I hope you haven't caught my sore throat.'

'There is something else, something unpleasant, that I must tell you.' Emma paused, taking a deep breath. 'I have been grossly mistaken, Harriet, in Mr Elton's intentions. Mr Elton, while respecting you greatly, has revealed that it is I instead who have caught his fancy. And I, who have never seen him in any regard but as an admirer of you, am mortified by my misjudgement.'

A tear fell down Harriet's cheek and Emma felt a renewed sense of shame. She reiterated her embarrassment, blaming herself for everything, but Harriet smiled through her tears, telling Miss Woodhouse that no one was to blame.

'I cannot complain,' she told Emma. 'For it seems impossible that a gentleman of Mr Elton's standing would consider me. I could never have deserved him. Only so kind a friend as you, Miss Woodhouse, would have thought it possible.'

In that moment, it seemed to Emma that she had been wrong to think that she might have anything to teach Harriet about the world, for Harriet was so humble, so gracious despite her misery, that she was surely the superior of the two.

'In time, we will drive him from your thoughts,' Emma assured her.

'Yes,' Harriet said, her voice wavering. 'Although, a gentleman so perfect as Mr Elton will be difficult to forget. I will be sure to see him a lot in Highbury and I will have to bear his company the best I can, considering him only ... only an acquaintance and nothing more.'

At that, Harriet's face crumpled. Emma could do nothing but grasp her hands in hers, as the tears continued to fall.

CHAPTER ELEVEN

No matter how she tried, Emma could not get Mr Elton out of Harriet's head.

She attempted various activities to keep Harriet busy, but nothing worked. Mr Elton would inevitably be mentioned at some point and Harriet's mood would drop once again.

'Have you heard the news?' Emma said one morning as they walked. 'Frank Churchill is not coming any more.'

'Oh dear, that is a shame,' Harriet said, looking as though she did not care so much. Suddenly she stopped and grabbed Emma's arm.

'What is it?' Emma asked.

'Look.' Harriet nodded at the ground, her eyes glistening with tears.

Emma followed her gaze and could see nothing but dirt and a few pebbles.

'There,' Harriet said, pointing at an old lace trodden into the ground so it was barely visible. 'A boot lace!'

'What about it?' Emma asked, baffled.

'Don't you remember?' Harriet croaked. 'Your boot lace broke when we were walking together with Mr Elton. You had to stop and let us walk ahead.'

'Yes, dear, but that was a different lane! We are miles from there, I don't think this can be that same boot lace.'

'No, but seeing this boot lace reminded me of that other boot lace.' Harriet sniffed, her eyes downcast. 'And that in turn reminded me of Mr Elton.'

Emma persuaded her to keep walking on and as Harriet stole wistful looks over her shoulder back at the boot lace, Emma knew that she'd have to think of something better to distract Harriet from Mr Elton than pleasant country walks and entertaining conversation. She had been sure that the topic of Frank Churchill would work, as it was all anyone else could talk about.

Even Mr Knightley had spoken about it at length, in such a manner that had surprised Emma. She knew Mr Knightley had his doubts about the man, but during their conversation, she had come to the conclusion that Mr Knightley was determined to dislike him.

'If Frank Churchill wanted to visit his father, he would come and visit him,' Mr Knightley had stated earlier that day. 'He is making excuses.'

Emma had laughed. 'How do you know that he is making excuses?'

'We know that he visited Weymouth recently. Did not he say so in his letter to Mrs Weston? And yet his aunt cannot spare him so that he may come to Highbury! It is impossible. He only goes to places when it is worth his while and uses the Churchills as an excuse when he chooses.'

'Mr Knightley, it is unfair to judge him. You do not know that his aunt hasn't demanded he stay with her at this time, but didn't the time he went to Weymouth.'

'Emma, there is one thing which a man can always do, and that is his duty. He is either idle and does not want to come, or he is weak in not standing up to his aunt and reminding her that he has a duty to his father.'

Emma had found the whole conversation both entertaining and astonishing. That Mr Knightley should take such a dislike to Frank Churchill without even meeting him seemed at odds with his character. Mr Knightley had often guided Emma to realise and regret her swift judgements and prejudices! It was quite hypocritical of him.

She was just thinking of telling Harriet about Mr Knightley's curious opinions on Frank Churchill in the hope that it may help overcome the power of that old boot lace, when another solution presented itself. They came upon the house where Mrs and Miss Bates lived. There was no chance of Harriet having the opportunity to get upset in there.

'Harriet, we are going to pay a visit on Miss Bates,' Emma said, taking her arm and steering her in the direction of their front door.

Miss Bates was overwhelmed with happiness to see them and thanked them so many times and in so many ways for the honour of stopping by, that Emma was very tempted to make an excuse to leave at once.

'You just missed Mrs Cole,' Miss Bates told them, offering them cake while Mrs Bates sat silently knitting by the fire. 'And can you guess who she had news of?'

Emma did not know who, nor did she care to guess. She did not associate with people such as Mr and Mrs Cole, who had made their money through trade. Acquiring new wealth earned them a fairly respectable social status, but it did not make them members of the truly genteel class.

'You cannot guess who Mrs Cole spoke of? Then I shall tell you, Miss Woodhouse! She spoke of Mr Elton!' Miss Bates exclaimed. 'Yes, he's in Bath, you see, and you may know that he and Mr Cole are particular friends.'

'Ah, yes,' Emma said, glancing in concern over to Harriet, who was nibbling her cake with a glum expression.

'The toast of the town, Mrs Cole said!' Miss Bates continued. 'Of course he is, I said, for Mr Elton is the toast of Highbury, too! He is doing well on the card tables and been to all the balls! Apparently the Master of the Ceremonies' ball was very full. Mr Elton, I daresay, danced with many young ladies.'

As Miss Bates prattled on, Emma could only stare at her slice of dry cake in mortification. This was more disastrous than she could have imagined. Thankfully, Miss Bates moved the topic off Mr Elton and began to speak of her niece, Jane Fairfax.

Usually this would have been an unwelcome change for Emma, but today, for Harriet's sake, she was delighted to hear of dull Jane Fairfax and all her accomplishments, so long as Mr Elton was not mentioned any further.

'Jane is coming to Highbury!' Miss Bates cried, searching for the letter from Jane she had just received. 'She will come here for three months as the Campbells, her guardians, are off to visit their daughter and her new husband in Ireland.'

'Mr and Mrs Dixon?'

'Yes! Miss Woodhouse, you are quite correct! How clever you are! How kind to remember! Mother and I always say how kind you are, Miss Woodhouse, there is no one as kind as you. How did you know of Mr and Mrs Dixon in Ireland? How clever you are to know of them!'

'I have had the pleasure of listening to you talk of them before. I recall that Jane gets on very well with the Campbells' daughter, Mrs Dixon?'

'Yes! Yes, that is right! How sweet you are to remember. Yes, now Miss Campbell is Mrs Dixon and moved to Ireland with Mr Dixon. Jane used to walk with them when they were courting!'

'I wonder that Jane does not go to visit Mr and

Mrs Dixon at their new home in Ireland, if they were so very close.'

'Yes! I wonder that myself, indeed. Mr Dixon saved Jane's life, you know. Yes, they were once out on the water at Weymouth and what should happen, but a gust of wind, a very bad gust of wind and oh! The thought of it makes me feel quite dizzy. Yes, I must sit down. Oh! I am already sitting down! How pleasant. Oh yes, the wind and the sails blustering about. Jane almost fell into the sea! It was Mr Dixon who grabbed her and prevented her from going in!'

A suspicion floated into Emma's head. Maybe the reason why Jane had not gone to Ireland was because she secretly loved Mr Dixon, her friend's new husband! Emma smiled to herself at this scandalous theory.

It would certainly make Jane Fairfax a *little* interesting.

CHAPTER TWELVE

'Jane Fairfax is completely impossible!'

Emma made her abrupt declaration to the surprise of Mr Knightley, who had been walking alongside her in the garden and in the middle of talking about bees.

'But I asked you your opinion of Miss Fairfax after we spent the evening with her and you remarked that she was very accomplished and that was it,' he noted.

'Yes, well, I was being polite,' Emma said, tugging at her gloves. 'And she *is* very accomplished.'

'And the reason for this sudden outburst?'

'I could not contain it any longer,' Emma

justified with a huff. 'I keep thinking about all the pleasant things you have said about her and I cannot agree.'

Mr Knightley attempted to suppress a smile at her tone. 'And what, may I ask, has Miss Fairfax done to provoke such negative feeling?'

'She is too reserved. She wouldn't answer any question properly! You know she met Frank Churchill in Weymouth? I asked her whether he was handsome and her answer was, "Some say he is handsome." Then I asked if he was agreeable, to which she replied, "Many found his manners pleasing." Really! I couldn't get a bit of real information from her!'

'Is it so important to you to hear of Frank Churchill?'

'That is not the point; the point is that she would not give me any real information on anything! She was so quiet and cold. I cannot forgive her.'

'Emma,' Mr Knightley chuckled, 'consider that, for her, she was in *your* home amongst new society. Can you not allow her to be shy or a little overwhelmed?'

'She is not that new to Highbury. She has been visiting her aunt ever since she was a girl. We have been forced into each other's company many times.'

'I do not think she felt forced into anything. She appeared grateful to be in so grand a house as Hartfield and invited by you to play the pianoforte. She cannot have such a luxury at her aunt's house.'

'Oh yes.' Emma rolled her eyes. 'You would mention her *superior* piano playing.'

'You played beautifully, too.'

'Not compared to Miss Fairfax,' Emma observed, pursing her lips.

Mr Knightley watched her, giving a sly smile. 'You're *jealous*.'

Emma blinked at him. 'What?'

'You're jealous of Miss Fairfax.' Mr Knightley laughed. 'You are used to everyone admiring your beauty and your accomplishments, and now you fear that Miss Fairfax will be the talk of Highbury gossips.'

'Do not be absurd!' Emma scowled at him. 'Jealous of Miss Fairfax? She may be nice to look at, I admit, but that is about it. How can I be jealous of someone who has no claims of inheritance and is soon to become a governess?'

'Precisely so,' Mr Knightley said in a serious tone. 'You cannot be jealous when Jane Fairfax deserves your compassion and generous friendship.'

Emma was quiet and then said, 'Anyway, I hope she had a pleasant evening.'

Mr Knightley smiled kindly at her as they approached the house. 'She did. You gave her a warm welcome. Now, before I go home to Donwell Abbey, I need to tell you something I heard this morning—'

Mr Knightley was cut off on entering the house by Miss Bates, who had stopped by Hartfield with Jane Fairfax to thank Emma for sending them a hindquarter of pork that morning.

'There you are, Miss Woodhouse! And Mr Knightley! In from the cold! You have done well to walk so early as it is about to rain, I am sure! On the way here, did not I say, Jane, that it looked as though it might rain? For there were those dark clouds! Oh, Miss Woodhouse, I was just thanking your father for the pork you kindly sent us. To be blessed with such generous friends! It is the best pork we shall ever taste; I am quite sure of it!'

'I am delighted—'

'Have you heard the news indeed? Such wonderful news! Oh, said I to Mrs Cole, it is lovely news that shall warm our hearts! Mr Elton to be married so quickly! How charming. Miss Hawkins is her name. They met in Bath but four weeks ago! For he has only been there four weeks, as you know, Miss Woodhouse.'

'Mr Elton, married?' Mr Woodhouse chimed from the fireplace. 'Poor Mr Elton! He always loved to spend time here and now he is married, he will not be able to visit so often.'

'We must be getting back to Mother, for she will be wondering where we are, Jane!' Miss Bates announced in a frenzy, before saying her goodbyes, which took a good ten minutes, and leaving. Jane trailed after her without saying a word during the entire exchange.

'And there you have it,' Mr Knightley said, smiling to Emma, 'the news I was about to reveal to you. Mr Elton is married.'

Emma had been too stunned to comment. At least it confirmed Mr Elton had not loved her so much that he could not fall in love with and marry someone else within four weeks. But Emma thought of Harriet and how this would hurt her.

As Miss Bates promised, it began to rain. Mr Knightley left to go home and soon after, the light shower became heavier. Then, just as it began to wane, Harriet Smith appeared at Hartfield, soaked through. She had clearly been caught in the downpour without an umbrella.

'Miss Woodhouse, you won't believe what I have to tell you,' she burst out before Emma could even greet her.

'You have heard,' Emma said gravely, guiding her to the warmth of the fire.

'Heard what?'

'Oh, um, nothing. What were you saying?'

'I set out for Hartfield,' Harriet began, removing her bonnet, her wet curls plastered against her face, 'and as it began to rain, I ran into a shop to look at ribbons and buttons. Who should dash in just behind me? Miss Elizabeth Martin and her brother, Mr Martin! I thought I was going to faint! What do you think I did?'

'What did you do?'

'I hid!'

'You hid?'

'Yes, Miss Woodhouse, I hid. Very well too, I ducked behind a row of blue patterned cloth. And what do you think happened then?'

'They did not see you and left the shop?'

'They DID see me and they did NOT leave the shop! They came over to talk to me! I do not think they knew I was hiding, though. I made out I was looking at the pattern of the cloth very close.'

'I am sure they were convinced.'

'Oh, Miss Woodhouse, they were so very kind to me.' She let out a long sigh. 'I thought they would be angry and awkward, but they were so friendly. Miss Elizabeth Martin said she was sorry I did not see her as often now. And then, when I left to come here, Mr Martin ran after me and told me that the path to Hartfield was flooded, so I should go round the stables way. Wasn't that kind?'

Emma agreed it was kind. Harriet's story brought forth a surprising wave of guilt. The way Mr Martin behaved showed he had real feeling for Harriet and sadness at losing her.

But then, Emma considered, he may just have been sorry to lose her because marrying Harriet would have brought him into higher society. Yes, that was more likely the reason than real affection for her.

As Harriet continued to talk of Mr Martin with a giddy smile, Emma became concerned. They did not want a relapse into her caring for Mr Martin simply because he warned her of a flooded path. There was a certain way to take her mind firmly off Mr Martin.

'Harriet,' Emma began gently, sitting her down, 'I have some news to tell you. Some news of Mr Elton.'

CHAPTER THIRTEEN

Mr Elton's marriage soon became overshadowed by something much more exciting: Mr Frank Churchill was coming to Highbury at last.

The timing could not have been better in Emma's mind. She and Harriet had been in the middle of some very unpleasant business – Harriet had been at Hartfield the day before and returned home to discover that Miss Elizabeth Martin had called to see her.

She would have to return the visit, as to not do so would have been improper and unpardonably rude. Harriet was distressed at the possibility of seeing Mr Martin and Emma was irritated that the

Martins insisted on keeping a connection with Harriet. A plan was formed by Miss Woodhouse that solved all problems: Harriet *would* return the visit, but briefly. Emma would drop her at their farm in the carriage and pick her up fifteen minutes later.

'They were very upset at me having to leave so quickly,' Harriet was telling Emma in the carriage, after the agreed fifteen minutes were up. She wrung her hands together anxiously. 'They must think I'm so rude! They must believe that I think they are beneath me.'

They are *beneath you, dear*, Emma thought.

Their carriage came to a halt as Mr and Mrs Weston walked by and stopped to tell them the news of Frank Churchill's impending visit.

'He is coming tomorrow,' Mrs Weston enthused, squeezing her husband's arm. 'We shall bring him to Hartfield the following day to meet you.'

'We are eager for you to meet him, Miss Woodhouse,' Mr Weston said with great feeling. 'I very much hope you will like him.'

Mr and Mrs Weston's hopeful looks and comments whenever Frank Churchill was mentioned in Emma's company had not gone unnoticed. It was known among Highbury residents that Emma and Frank Churchill was a much wished-for match. Both handsome, wealthy and well-thought-of, it made sense to all involved.

Emma was thinking about Frank Churchill the next day as she walked down the stairs from her bedroom, wondering if he might be the one to change her mind about marriage, when she opened the parlour door to find Mr Weston and a young man beside him sitting with her father.

'Miss Woodhouse,' Mr Weston said, jumping to his feet at once. 'May I present my son, Frank Churchill.'

Emma could not hide the joy she felt at finally meeting someone who had been talked of all her life and it appeared that joy was reciprocated. He bowed his head to her, smiling broadly.

Frank Churchill met all expectations. He was *very* good looking and, Emma noted at once, had most acceptable sideburns just as she'd imagined. Their first conversation proved that he was charm itself. He said how honoured he was to meet Miss Woodhouse, went on about how beautiful the village was, and concluded that it was very good to come home at last. On hearing the last comment, Mr Weston puffed out his chest like a proud peacock.

'My father intends to show me around Highbury tomorrow,' he said, before bringing his eyes up to meet Emma's. 'I wonder, Miss Woodhouse; would you do me the honour of joining us?'

Emma replied that she would be happy to, ignoring Mr Weston's exultant expression as he witnessed the exchange.

Walking through Highbury the next day, Mr and Mrs Weston fell naturally behind and Emma was left to walk next to Frank. Their conversation flowed easily. They had a similar sense of humour and Emma had to admit that she greatly enjoyed his company. She thought him to be a welcome addition to her circle of friends.

'I visited Miss Bates yesterday, just after we left you,' Frank informed her. 'I'm not sure if you're aware but I met her niece in Weymouth briefly

and felt I should call on her. I forget her name ...'

'Miss Jane Fairfax,' Emma said. 'She is very accomplished.'

'That is it. Yes, she is accomplished, but very plain.'

Emma looked at him in surprise. 'I cannot agree, sir! Miss Fairfax cannot be described as plain.

Perhaps her character may not be to your taste and it affects your judgement of her appearance.'

'Perhaps.' He hesitated, offering her a knowing smile. 'And what do you think of her character, Miss Woodhouse?'

'What do *you* think of her character, Mr Frank Churchill?'

Frank laughed. 'I think she is ... reserved. She says very little.'

'That is just what I think,' Emma agreed.

'In Weymouth, she was a little more open. She was amongst her friends there, Miss Campbell and Mr Dixon. Mr and Mrs Dixon, I should say now. I believe it is said that Miss Fairfax particularly excels in music – have you heard her play and sing?'

'I have,' Emma replied.

'And what did you think?'

'She plays charmingly.'

Frank nodded. 'I wanted your opinion because I have heard enough of your own musical talent to know that you could be a proper judge. Of course, I have heard her complimented many times before. Her friend, Mr Dixon, often spoke of her talent.'

Emma was amused. 'Is that so?'

'Yes, he was engaged to Miss Campbell at the time, but he would never ask her to play. Only Miss Fairfax, which must prove that she is very talented indeed.'

'Poor Mrs Dixon! She must have felt hurt by Mr Dixon's preference?'

Frank looked confused for a moment. 'I do not think so. She appreciates Miss Fairfax is exceptionally talented.'

'Well, then, I am sure Miss Fairfax felt embarrassed.' Emma smiled, her eyes twinkling with mischief. 'No wonder she did not go to Ireland where she may be considered a danger to her friend.'

It dawned on Frank what Emma was implying and he raised his eyebrows. 'I do not know them so well as to guess what was going on behind the scenes. You would be a better judge, Miss Woodhouse, knowing Miss Fairfax a lot better than I do.'

They had come to the Crown Inn and stopped there so that Mr Weston could tell his son of its history. It had been built to be a ballroom for Highbury and had been very popular a long time ago. Now, such dancing days were over for the neighbourhood and it had been left unused.

'Why are the dancing days over for Highbury?' Frank asked curiously, peering through the window at the ballroom. 'It looks like a splendid space for a ball!'

'There are not enough proper people in Highbury to fill it,' Emma informed him.

'Nonsense! Just looking down this street I see enough people to ensure I have a wonderful time at a ball,' he declared, his eyes flickering to Emma, who felt them upon her and blushed.

Mr and Mrs Weston also noticed and shared a hopeful look.

'Miss Woodhouse,' Frank continued, 'we all know that you are the only person in Highbury who could bring this ballroom back to its former glory. If Miss Woodhouse wanted a ball, there would be a ball.'

Emma burst out laughing. 'You flatter me, sir.'

'Would not you agree, Father? Do you not think Highbury deserves a ball?'

'I do agree,' Mr Weston chuckled. 'And if Miss Woodhouse wants one, I would be happy to organise it in both your honours.'

'So, Miss Woodhouse,' Frank said, grinning at her, 'what do you say? Will there be music in Highbury again? Or will the village be doomed to never enjoy the English country dance again?'

'As you wish it.' Emma laughed. 'I declare there shall be a ball!'

CHAPTER FOURTEEN

'I hear Frank Churchill has persuaded his father to organise a ball,' Mr Knightley said later that week. 'You have heard of it, I'm sure.'

'Of course,' Emma replied. 'I was there when the idea presented itself. We still need to set a date for it.'

'I am not fond of dancing.'

'I know that.'

'Did you know Frank Churchill travelled all the way to London the other day just for a haircut?' Mr Knightley shook his head in disbelief. 'Mr Weston must be mortified by his son's vanity. Frank Churchill is exactly the silly fellow I expected him to be.'

Emma only smiled. She did in fact agree with Mr Knightley. This whim of Frank's seemed ridiculous to her, but she did not want to admit it and gratify her companion.

'I suppose,' Mr Knightley continued, 'he will insist on dancing at the Coles's party. It is the sort of thing he'd do, even though no one else would want it.'

This grabbed Emma's attention. Was Mr Knightley possibly considering attending a party hosted by Mr and Mrs Cole, those newly wealthy friends of Mr Elton and Miss Bates? Surely not. He would not associate with a family who had made their money in *trade*.

Would he?

'The Coles's party? I did not think *you* would be invited,' Emma noted. 'We certainly haven't been. Of course, I would have to decline any invitation from the Coles.'

'My invitation arrived yesterday and I have accepted it.'

Emma blinked at him. She knew that Mr and Mrs Cole were hosting a party but, being greatly beneath Emma in social status, she also knew they should never presume to invite her. It would not be proper to invite the *superior* families of Highbury, like the Woodhouses. But Mr Knightley, if anything, ranked higher than the Woodhouses! His home, Donwell Abbey, was certainly the better and bigger estate.

'Well!' Emma huffed, forgetting herself. 'That they should invite you and not me is a great insult.'

'You just said that you would have to decline them.'

'I would! But I would like to have the opportunity to decline them!'

'You want them to invite you just so you can refuse them?'

Emma hesitated. Mr Knightley had a very

irritating way of saying things in a manner that made her look bad.

'They should either invite neither of us or both of us,' Emma concluded, avoiding his eye contact. 'Their conduct is appalling. I shall never be tempted to go to any gathering at the Coles's again.'

The invitation from the Coles arrived moments later. At first, Emma was determined to stick to her word and told Mr Knightley so, but when she mentioned the invitation to Mrs Weston and Frank Churchill later that day, they were so persuasive about her going to the party that she decided to accept. Reluctantly. The Coles were very lucky they had caught her in such a generous mood.

On the evening of the party, Emma had only just walked into the room when she was swept to the side by Frank Churchill.

'Have you heard this fascinating news of Miss Fairfax?' he asked in excitement. 'She has been sent a surprise gift! A pianoforte.'

'Goodness! Who sent her such a generous gift?'

'That is why I smile,' he said, keeping his voice low. 'It is a mystery! There was no note. At first, everyone thought it must be her guardians, the Campbells, but it was not from them. Everyone in Highbury is talking of it, making guesses as to who it might be.'

'From your teasing expression, I am guessing you have a theory?'

'What say you to it being *Mr Dixon*?'

Emma gasped. 'It cannot be. He is married to her friend!'

'But you put the idea in my head! What if he fell hopelessly in love with Miss Fairfax? He saved her from falling overboard into the sea, did he not?'

Emma nodded. 'Perhaps the pianoforte is from Mr *and* Mrs Dixon. Mrs Dixon knows Miss Fairfax is fond of music.'

'Perhaps,' he said, before adding, 'but then why would they keep it secret?'

They were interrupted by Mrs Weston, and Frank Churchill excused himself to mingle with others at the party. Emma saw that he made his way over to where Jane Fairfax was standing with Miss Bates.

'Have you heard about Miss Fairfax?' Mrs Weston began, noticing Emma's line of sight.

'Yes, I daresay she will get great use out of a pianoforte.'

'I was not speaking of the mystery pianoforte; I was speaking of Mr Knightley.'

Emma turned to her. 'What of Mr Knightley?'

'Did you know that he sent his carriage to collect Miss Bates and Miss Fairfax to bring them to the party tonight?' Mrs Weston said, raising her eyebrows.

'I did not, but that doesn't surprise me. Mr Knightley is exceedingly thoughtful and he knows that they cannot afford a carriage and have to walk to occasions such as this. It is cold out.'

'An idea has struck me,' Mrs Weston confided in excitement. 'What do you think about Mr Knightley and Jane Fairfax as a match?'

'*What?*' Emma had to stop herself from laughing rudely at her friend. 'Mr Knightley and Jane Fairfax? Impossible!'

'Why impossible?'

'For a start, he could not be interested in her. She barely talks! And Mr Knightley is so intelligent and ... Well, he would not want to spend his evenings with her. And for another thing, she is to be a governess! Leave the matchmaking to me, Mrs Weston, I'm not sure you have an eye for it.'

'Her being a governess would not put him off if he loves her,' Mrs Weston pointed out. 'He does not need to marry into any money.' She paused before adding, 'Perhaps it was Mr Knightley who sent her the mystery pianoforte!'

'Mrs Weston, please!' Emma scoffed. 'Mr Knightley would never think to do such a romantic gesture for anyone! Let alone Jane Fairfax.'

'Are you quite certain?' Mrs Weston said. 'Well, let us see how this evening plays out. Gentlemen, *any* gentleman, can be surprising when they are in love.'

Emma could not get it off her mind for the rest

of the party. Mr Knightley and Jane Fairfax? Impossible! Simply impossible! Just the thought of such a bad match was giving Emma a headache.

When Mr Knightley fell into conversation with Jane Fairfax after dinner, Emma stared at them intently. She was trying to make out if Mr Knightley was enjoying the experience or not.

At one point, he laughed. Laughed! It was insufferable behaviour! It must be politeness. Yes, Mr Knightley was surely just being polite. Emma could not think of anything that Jane Fairfax would have to say that would be in the *least* bit amusing.

Emma watched as Mr Knightley excused himself from Miss Fairfax's company and caught Emma's eye, moving across the room towards her. She quickly pretended to be busy studying the drawing-room curtains.

'Ah, Mr Knightley!' Emma said, as he approached. 'I did not see you there. I was just ... admiring this curtain.'

The corners of Mr Knightley's mouth twitched. 'It is a charming colour.'

'How kind it was of you to send your carriage for Miss Fairfax this evening! I wish I had thought of sending my carriage for their convenience.'

'I did not like to think of anyone walking in the cold,' he said simply.

'What do you think of this pianoforte business?'

'The one sent to Jane? I don't approve of surprises. I suspect it was the Campbells who sent it.' He paused, watching Emma curiously. 'Why do you smile? You look very pleased with yourself, which is always worrying.'

'I don't know what you mean,' she replied, in a much better mood.

Emma was satisfied with this answer. Mrs Weston was completely off; it was clear that Mr Knightley had no affection for Jane Fairfax.

CHAPTER FIFTEEN

Emma stood over the mystery pianoforte. Jane Fairfax, Miss Bates, Mrs Bates, Harriet, Mrs Weston and Frank Churchill were all in the room, waiting in silence for Miss Woodhouse's opinion, the opinion that mattered the most.

'It is truly a magnificent instrument,' Emma announced.

Jane Fairfax looked greatly relieved and Miss Bates instantly launched into a ramble about the

excellent taste of Miss Woodhouse. When Miss Bates paused for breath, Frank Churchill spoke, offering a knowing smile to Emma.

'Such a magnificent instrument can only have been sent in true affection.'

The result of his comment was the blushing of two ladies: Miss Fairfax and Emma herself, who was embarrassed that Frank was openly teasing Jane and wished that he wouldn't. In fact, she was beginning to regret telling him her silly theory about Mr Dixon and Jane Fairfax.

'We are all so excited at the prospect of a ball,' Miss Bates said. 'Mother has been talking of nothing else!'

The others looked doubtfully at Mrs Bates, who was fast asleep in her chair with her mouth hanging open.

'Are you looking forward to the ball, Miss Fairfax?' Mrs Weston asked kindly.

'Oh yes.' Jane Fairfax smiled. 'I very much hope

it goes ahead.'

'Of course it shall go ahead!' Frank Churchill cried. 'Miss Woodhouse has said it shall, and we cannot disappoint Miss Woodhouse. She has promised me the first dance.'

Emma laughed. Jane Fairfax looked down at her hands and did not say any more.

'Mr Weston is determined that all shall go to plan. We are hoping it shall be next week,' Mrs Weston informed them cheerily.

'Look!' Harriet said, glancing out the window. 'It is Mr Knightley going by.'

'Mr Knightley, I declare! Oh! I must speak to him at once,' Miss Bates insisted, throwing open the window, letting all the cold air in to call out to him. 'Mr Knightley! Hello there! Oh you look so handsome on horseback! Do come in! Do come in!'

'I am on my way to Kingston, so cannot stop. While I am there can I get you anything?' they heard him call back.

'So obliging! So obliging, Mr Knightley! There is nothing we need, thank you, sir. But will not you come in from the cold? Some of your friends are here! Miss Smith and Miss Woodhouse!'

'Perhaps I will come in; I can spare five minutes.'

'And Mrs Weston and Frank Churchill! Come in! So many friends!'

'No, thank you, I must be going. I cannot stop, I must get to Kingston as fast as I can.'

'Mr Knightley, I must thank you before you go for the apples you sent us for Jane. You heard her say she liked them and then who should show up this morning? Your servant with the apples from your orchard. Thank you, sir! Good day, sir!'

Mrs Weston gave Emma a knowing look at the mention of the apples, but Emma just shook her head stubbornly. Although Emma believed it was nothing more than Mr Knightley being thoughtful, she felt a strange sensation at the mention of these apples he had sent specifically for Jane. She suddenly felt a little unwell. She managed to excuse herself and Harriet shortly after, and went home wondering if this uncomfortable feeling was something to do with the stew she'd had the night before.

Over the next few days, all of Highbury was preoccupied with the upcoming ball. Frank Churchill was considered the most charming man in the country to have thought up such an idea. The only person who did not wish to speak of it was Mr Knightley. He frowned at any mention of it and kept saying things like, 'I would much rather stay at home.'

But one morning, Frank Churchill arrived at Hartfield to tell Emma some grave news while her father was doing his daily turn about the garden.

'I must return to my aunt. She has fallen very sick and needs me at her side at once.'

Emma was stunned. 'When are you leaving?'

'This very morning.'

'But ...' Emma searched for words, unprepared for such upheaval. 'The ball!'

'I cannot bear it!' he cried dramatically, pacing the room. 'I have been so happy in Hartfield! And now to leave it! What shall we do about the ball?'

Emma was indeed disappointed at the news, but felt that Frank Churchill was being a tad dramatic. To flail his arms about in such a manner was unnecessary and put a host of valuable vases perched about the room in great danger.

'We can postpone the ball until you return,' Emma suggested calmly.

'Yes, that will have to do. Miss Woodhouse, you will not forget that you promised me the first dance.'

'I shall remember.'

Frank Churchill continued pacing about the room and Emma began to wonder that he did not have something else he wished to say. He seemed in such a frenzy at having to leave and it could not possibly just be down to the matter of postponing a ball.

'Are you going to say goodbye to Miss Bates and Miss Fairfax?' Emma asked as he walked about deep in thought. She didn't like the silence and it was the only thing she could think of to say.

He looked up at her intently. 'I stopped there on the way here.'

'Oh!' Emma was a little surprised. After all, Hartfield should really have been his first port of call in the proper sense, but she supposed the Bates's house was on the way to Hartfield.

'Miss Woodhouse,' he said, coming towards her, 'I think you already may have a suspicion—'

He hesitated. It came upon Emma that he might be about to confess his love for her! He certainly seemed like he had something to say that was of the utmost importance. She supposed she should rally herself for the declaration, but wasn't sure how one was meant to act in such a situation. Should she sit down? Stay standing? Start blushing? Look out of the window in a dreamy sort of way? Oh bother, why hadn't she read up about this?

'Miss Woodhouse,' he began breathlessly, 'I must tell you—'

The doors opened and Mr Weston was announced. It was time for Frank to go. He smiled with a look of regret, said 'Goodbye' and was gone.

Emma sighed and sat down. Frank Churchill was in love with her. He was about to say so before they had been interrupted. She wondered if she was in love with him, too. She would miss seeing him every day to be sure, as he was lively and cheerful, and she felt a bit weary today, so perhaps she was in love with him after all.

One thing she could be sure of was that the loss of the ball would be greatly mourned, by herself and all those in Highbury.

She smiled. Except Mr Knightley, of course.

CHAPTER SIXTEEN

On meeting the new Mrs Elton, Emma thought she was very elegantly dressed. After two minutes of talking to her, Emma thought she was quite vain. And after five minutes, Emma thought she was quite possibly the most vulgar woman in the country.

'Your grounds are very neat,' Mrs Elton commented, gesturing out the window. 'Hartfield reminds me of my sister's estate, Maple Grove – she married Mr Suckling, you know, a *very* wealthy gentleman. He would be enchanted by this place. People of extensive grounds are always pleased with anyone of extensive grounds!'

Emma could only smile graciously.

'They have a *barouche-landau*, you know,' Mrs Elton said with great emphasis, giving her a knowing look. Emma realised she was supposed to be impressed. 'Only the best will do. It's a very preferable carriage.'

Tea was brought in and Emma invited her to sit down.

'You must come to Bath, Miss Woodhouse,' Mrs Elton sighed, stirring her tea. 'I should be happy to introduce you there and, you know, that would secure you the best society in the place.'

It took all of Emma's energy not to laugh at such a suggestion. Mrs Elton had fooled herself into thinking they were of equal standing. Not only was her situation inferior to Emma's, but her manners appalling. She was self-satisfied, overly familiar and deeply ignorant. Her conceited, obvious pride in her sister's advantageous marriage was also in very bad taste. Mr Elton had chosen poorly for himself.

'I hear you play the pianoforte delightfully, Miss Woodhouse. I am passionately fond of music. We must create a musical society together! I said as much to Mr E!'

Mr E? She called him Mr E!

'I must say, dear Miss Woodhouse, I foresee us spending a lot of time together,' Mrs Elton chuckled, sipping her tea loudly. 'For I have been used to a much bigger house than Mr E's. I am very comfortable here at Hartfield; the size of the rooms is more to my taste.'

Emma picked up her teacup from the saucer and made a non-committal 'mm' sound that Mrs Elton took as an enthusiastic agreement.

'Oh! I must tell you, I met Mr and Mrs Weston! Well.' Mrs Elton put down her tea cup and looked wide-eyed at Emma. 'Mrs Weston is a lot more *lady-like* than I thought she would be. She was your governess, wasn't she? I was shocked to find her well-mannered! She has done *very* well to become quite the gentlewoman!'

Emma was at a loss as to what to say.

'And who do you think was there when we visited,' Mrs Elton continued, oblivious to her insults, 'Knightley! Quite the gentleman. He is very handsome. I wonder that he is not married. He will be a good catch.'

She had gone too far. *Knightley?* Knightley! Even to call a gentleman one had known all their life by their surname without using a title would be improper, and she'd only just met him!

'My dear Miss Woodhouse, I am so very fond of Jane Fairfax. Such a talented young woman and I feel deeply sorry that she will become a governess and drop from all good society. Until such a time comes, I have decided to take her under my wing.' At this, Mrs Elton leaned forwards to Emma as though sharing a secret. 'We must do so together. For if *we* show fondness towards Jane Fairfax, the rest of Highbury society will follow. Then, she can at least have a pleasant time amongst civil society until she finds a governess position.'

To Emma's surprise, Mr Elton seemed to be proud of his wife, showing her off as though he'd done

Highbury a great credit in bringing her there. Mrs Elton made good on her promise and gave Jane Fairfax more attention than would be expected of her. Emma thought Miss Fairfax might shy away from it, and who would blame her? But it was not so – Miss Fairfax began to spend a lot of time with Mrs Elton.

'I cannot make her out,' Emma said, sitting one morning with Mrs Weston and Mr Knightley.

'Mrs Elton?' Mr Knightley raised his eyebrows. 'I wouldn't describe her as much of a mystery. I am fully aware of everything that she is exceedingly talented at, told to me by Mrs Elton herself.'

'Not Mrs Elton. Miss Fairfax,' Emma corrected. 'She has had another invitation from the Campbells and the Dixons to go to Ireland. She's refused it! Why would you not want to join your friends? Why stay here and suffer Mrs Elton?'

'Miss Fairfax is a sensible creature, my dear Emma,' Mrs Weston pointed out. 'She will have her reasons.'

'Miss Fairfax is capable of making her own judgements and she may enjoy the attention from Mrs Elton as she receives it from no one else,' Mr Knightley said, with a reproachful look at Emma.

Emma knew that she had not been as generous to Jane Fairfax as she perhaps should have been. But the woman could never give a decided opinion on anything, so how could Emma be expected to sit with her longer than a few minutes?

'We know how highly *you* think of Miss Fairfax, Mr Knightley,' Mrs Weston said pointedly, glancing at Emma.

Mr Knightley picked up on the insinuation and shifted in his seat.

'Anyone may know my regard for Miss Fairfax,' he said hurriedly.

'Perhaps,' Emma said with an arch look at him, 'you have more admiration for her than you know.'

Mr Knightley suddenly became very interested

in the lower buttons of his thick leather gaiters, his cheeks colouring.

'I can see what you are getting at and I can assure you that I have no interest in Miss Fairfax.' He hesitated, sitting straight again. 'Am I to believe that in your spirit of matchmaking, you have been settling that I should marry Miss Fairfax?'

'No!' Emma blurted out, before checking yourself. 'Certainly not. You could not come and sit with us in this comfortable way if you were married.'

'Good, then,' he replied. 'She is too reserved. I like an open temper.'

'I quite agree.'

There was silence and then Mr Knightley stood up and bowed, saying he had to get back to some important business at Donwell Abbey.

'You see, Mrs Weston?' Emma said triumphantly. 'He has no interest in Jane Fairfax. He is quite safe.'

'I disagree,' Mrs Weston replied. 'His words say one thing, his actions at our question another. I have never seen Mr Knightley blush before. I believe he is so much convinced he does not love her, that he *must* love her very much!'

CHAPTER SEVENTEEN

Emma was not in love with Frank Churchill.

She came to learn of this fact when she heard the news that after a few weeks he was returning to Highbury. Her heart did not beat any faster. She did not find herself breathless. And she realised she had not thought of Frank Churchill for some time.

She was happy to see him again but, along with everyone else in Highbury, she was even happier when Mr Weston announced that Frank's return heralded the chance to set the date of the ball. Frank returning at this time was another blessing for his father, as Mrs Weston had announced that she was pregnant.

The evening of the ball finally arrived and Emma set off in the carriage to pick up Harriet and bring her to the Crown Inn. Emma was dressed in her most exquisite, delicately embroidered white ball gown with a pretty headdress set within her fair curls, and Harriet was wearing a soft pink gown that, Emma noted, happily suited her complexion. Harriet could not contain her excitement at the prospect of a ball. While Emma sat demurely in the carriage, Harriet fidgeted and fretted over her perfectly arranged ringlets and the fan that Miss Woodhouse had lent her for the evening.

Frank Churchill was waiting by the door and, as the ladies entered in their finery, his eyes twinkled with joy. He looked particularly handsome in his black tail coat and fashionably high collar points, yet Emma's heart did not stir at the sight, confirming her suspicions. He was, she noticed, a little restless this evening.

'Miss Woodhouse, Miss Smith,' he said, bowing

his head. 'How lovely you both look.'

Emma noticed his eyes linger on Harriet's pretty face as she blushed, and an idea struck her. Harriet Smith and Frank Churchill! Now, there was a fine match.

'Ah!' he cried, looking past them. 'Miss Bates is here! I shall go and help her from the carriage!'

He darted past them and rushed to the carriage that had been sent by the Eltons to convey Miss Bates and Miss Fairfax to the ball, holding out an umbrella for them as it started to drizzle.

'Frank Churchill is so gallant,' Emma said to Harriet.

'Oh yes.' Harriet nodded, looking in awe at the ballroom and its finely dressed occupants. 'Very much so.'

What a shame that I must have the first dance with him, Emma thought. *I may be able to encourage him to ask Harriet for the second or third set.*

Mrs Elton, standing with Mrs Weston, greeted

them as they entered the main ballroom and Emma had to suppress a smile as she caught Mrs Weston's eye. It would seem that Mrs Elton felt it was as much her duty as Mrs Weston's to receive everyone on entering, as though it were *her* ball.

'Miss Woodhouse,' Mrs Elton said in a surprisingly cold tone, and completely overlooking Harriet, 'how do you do? You look very elegant.'

When Miss Fairfax entered the room on Frank Churchill's arm, Mrs Elton provided much more of a fanfare and Emma moved duly out of the way so poor Jane Fairfax might be bombarded by the empty compliments. Harriet was mortified and pleased to move into a quiet corner. Emma sighed, realising what must have happened for her and Harriet to receive such an icy greeting. Mr Elton had obviously let slip to his bride what occurred before he came to Bath and now she was determined to shun Harriet. He must have also told Mrs Elton of Emma's role in the misunderstanding.

'Miss Woodhouse,' Frank said, leaving Jane Fairfax and gliding across the room, his hand outstretched to her. 'The dancing is about to begin.'

All present in the ballroom could not help but notice such a handsome couple take their places on the floor. It would be talked of in Highbury for days after the ball – Miss Woodhouse was truly very beautiful, even lovelier than ever in her white evening gown, and there could not be a man so handsome as Frank Churchill. Their dancing was superior to the rest.

As she danced, Emma's thoughts were quite differently engaged. She had spotted Mr Knightley standing on the opposite side of the room. Why was he not dancing? She wished he would take some interest in it! For he looked very well tonight. He was speaking with an older gentleman and looked so tall and handsome next to his friend.

He caught her eye and smiled. Emma smiled back. She had better concentrate on her steps –

she noticed that Mr Knightley observed her for much of the dance and he was, no doubt, watching her critically.

The ball continued with great success. Laughter and music filled the room, and Emma's hand was so sought after, she had not sat down for one dance.

There was one person who was not having such a lovely time. Harriet Smith had not been asked to dance and Emma could not enjoy the ball so well, seeing her standing alone at the side. Thankfully, Mrs Weston noticed also and seeing Mr Elton was one of the only young men not engaged in dancing at present, moved next to him.

'Do not you dance, Mr Elton?'

'Most readily, Mrs Weston, if you will dance with me.'

'Ah, I do not mean to dance.'

'Perhaps I shall ask Mrs Gilbert over there. For though I am an old married man, it will give me great pleasure to dance with Mrs Gilbert!' He chuckled.

'Mrs Gilbert also does not mean to dance,' Mrs Weston said hurriedly, 'but there is a young lady disengaged! Miss Smith.'

Mr Elton's face fell. 'Oh. Miss Smith. I had not seen her there. Ah. You will excuse me. For if I were *not* an old married man, I would . . . As it is, I am an old married man. My dancing days are over.'

Harriet, who had heard every word, flushed a deep crimson. Mrs Weston was shocked at such a public slight. Emma could not bear to look. She continued to dance but grew hot with anger. Poor Harriet!

Emma's spirits were uplifted moments later, however, on seeing someone leading Harriet Smith to the line of dancers. She craned her neck to see who it was and thought her heart might burst with joy when she saw it was Mr Knightley! He threw himself into the dancing with admirable gusto and Harriet could not stop smiling as she danced with such an agreeable partner.

Emma sought him out after the dance and led him to a quiet corner so that they may speak over the music.

'Mr Elton was unpardonably rude,' Mr Knightley grumbled, after Emma praised him warmly for rescuing Harriet. 'It was a pleasure to stand up with her.'

'I see that you have been lying to me, Mr Knightley, for you are a superior dancer.'

He smiled before hesitating. 'I noticed that Mr and Mrs Elton seem to want to slight you, too, Emma.' He raised his eyebrows as she bowed her head. 'Confess, dear friend, that you *did* want him to marry Harriet.'

'I did. And it would seem they cannot forgive me. I was completely mistaken in Mr Elton and ignored all your warnings.'

'Let me say to make you feel better, that you chose much better for Mr Elton than he chose for himself,' Mr Knightley said gently. 'Harriet Smith has some first-rate qualities that Mrs Elton is completely without.'

'Miss Woodhouse!' Mr Weston cried, coming over to them. 'You should be dancing! You must set the example and all will follow.'

'I am ready, sir,' she replied, much to Mr Weston's satisfaction, who bustled away to find himself a partner.

'Who ... who are you going to dance with?' Mr Knightley asked curiously.

Emma hesitated, lifting her eyes to meet his. 'With you, if you will ask me.'

'Well, then.' He smiled and outstretched his hand. 'May I have this dance, Miss Woodhouse?'

CHAPTER EIGHTEEN

The morning after the ball, Emma was walking about the lawn smiling to herself about the evening's events, when the great iron sweep-gate opened and Harriet came through on the arm of Frank Churchill. Harriet was ghastly pale and frightened.

'Harriet, whatever is the matter?' Emma cried, hurrying to greet them.

'Miss Woodhouse,' Frank Churchill said, guiding Harriet towards the door. 'Let us sit her down and then we can tell the story in full. I think she may be about to—'

Before he could finish his sentence, Harriet fainted. He caught her and Emma helped him to bring her into the house, settling her into a chair. When Harriet recovered, her bright eyes filled with tears and Frank Churchill offered her his clean handkerchief.

'Oh, Mr Churchill,' Harriet sniffed. 'However can I thank you!'

'It is nothing,' he said, bowing his head towards her. 'I am only grateful that I chose to walk out slightly later this morning so that I happened upon you.'

'Miss Woodhouse, you would not believe it,' Harriet began. 'I was walking out with Miss Bickerton, another boarder at Mrs Goddard's. We had just reached the Richmond road when a traveller child ran up to us to beg! Miss Bickerton gave a great scream as he approached and ran away up a steep bank! She called on me to run away from him too, but I had a stich from dancing at the ball and could not follow. I was left alone to face him!'

Emma glanced at Frank Churchill, who kept his eyes to the floor.

'Left alone to face who, dear?'

'The small child!'

'You were left alone to face the small child?'

'It was terribly frightening!'

'The small child was terribly frightening?'

Harriet nodded vigorously. 'Oh yes.'

'And that is whom Mr Frank Churchill rescued you from?'

'There is more to the story, Miss Woodhouse,

it does not end there! I reached into my purse and gave the boy a coin, and then the rest of his family appeared from the trees! They asked if I had any more to spare. I thought I should faint then and there!'

'It was in this state that I found Miss Smith,' Frank Churchill said, as Harriet felt her forehead with the back of her hand.

'He frightened them away and brought me here,' Harriet said, her voice trembling. 'I will be for ever in your debt!'

'Do not speak of it,' he replied gently, smiling at her. 'I am glad that you are safe. And if I may, I must excuse myself for I am supposed to be with Miss Bates. I borrowed a pair of scissors from her the other day, you see, and I was on my way to return them.'

Assured by Emma that Harriet would be well taken care of, Frank set off and the rest of the morning was spent listening to Harriet relay the story several times, each time the number of begging children growing and by the fourth retelling, Harriet had been quite horribly attacked, left to die on the ground.

If the most unromantic person in the country had witnessed the spectacle of Frank Churchill appearing at Hartfield with a fainting Harriet on his arm, they would have surely declared these two were meant to be together. There was no reason now why they should not fall in love. Emma saw how Harriet looked at him, her brave rescuer, and how he looked back at her, the damsel in great need of his assistance.

Emma's suspicions were confirmed a few days later when Harriet arrived at Hartfield carrying a box with *Most Precious Treasures* written across the top.

'I have decided it is time to forget Mr Elton once and for all,' Harriet announced, leading Emma over to the chairs by the fire and sitting down confidently. 'There are two things that I have kept of Mr Elton's that I wish to destroy.'

'I am pleased to hear it, Harriet. His behaviour on returning to Highbury has proved that he never deserved you.'

'Well, I cannot think that, for he is a superior gentleman,' Harriet replied modestly. 'But I can now say that I have no feelings left for him, and I wish him and Mrs Elton well.'

'What gifts did he give you that you wish to get rid of?' Emma asked, looking at the box with great interest.

'They are not gifts. They are small treasures that I kept without his knowledge,' Harriet explained, opening it carefully. She pulled out what looked like a tiny, ragged piece of cloth.

'What is that?' Emma asked, squinting at it.

'Do you remember when Mr Elton cut his finger on the pen knife here at Hartfield one evening? You asked me to help him put a bandage on it. Well, I cut him a piece a bit too big, and once he'd dressed his finger this was the leftover bit.'

Emma blinked at her.

'Yes,' Harriet said gravely. 'A most precious treasure that means nothing to me now.'

Closing her eyes and inhaling deeply, Harriet threw the bit of bandage into the fire.

'Well done,' Emma said encouragingly.

Harriet pulled out the next treasure and held it aloft. It was a small bit of pencil.

'You must remember this, Miss Woodhouse.'

'Oh, um, I am not sure . . .'

'Do not you remember when Mr Knightley recommended to Mr Elton a type of beer? Mr Elton wished to make a note of it and he did so using this very pencil. Afterwards, I took this pencil and have never parted from it from that moment.'

Emma did not know what to say. It seemed all too ridiculous to her, but she did not want to appear unfeeling towards her friend, so she simply said, 'Oh, Harriet.'

'Yes,' she said in a solemn voice. 'Yes, it is time to let it go.'

She took a moment to gather the strength and then thrust it into the fire. The two ladies watched it become engulfed in flames. Harriet sat in silence and then spoke boldly.

'I shall never marry.'

'Harriet, do not make such a claim! You have moved on from Mr Elton. You just burned the plaster and the pencil.'

Harriet shook her head. 'It has nothing to do with Mr Elton. It has to do with' – she blushed – 'the one I can only think of marrying, who should never think of me.'

Emma instantly knew she was speaking of Frank Churchill and reached over to hold her hand in comfort. 'I shall not force you to speak your feelings, but do you say that because the gentleman in question is superior in situation?'

Harriet smiled gratefully at her friend. How lucky she was to have a friend like Miss Woodhouse, who was so clever she could read her mind!

'Yes,' she confessed. 'I am too much beneath him.'

'Harriet, I am not surprised at your feelings. How could you not admire such a man when he came to your rescue?'

'He rescued me from perfect misery and with him I was thrown into perfect happiness,' Harriet gushed. 'But, I must keep my feelings in check. I can at least admire him from a distance.'

'I think you are right to be cautious after we were so very wrong before. Let his actions guide your feelings.' Emma smiled kindly at her. 'Do not lose hope. For wonderful things can happen in life. Wonderful, unexpected things.'

CHAPTER NINETEEN

'You shall have to choose a wife for me, Miss Woodhouse,' Frank Churchill declared, sitting himself down next to Emma on the picnic blanket.

It was a beautiful sunny day in June and Mrs Elton had organised a party to travel to Box Hill, a delightful spot for a picnic. She had invited Mr and Mrs Weston and Frank Churchill, Miss Bates and dear Jane Fairfax, Miss Woodhouse and (reluctantly) Miss Smith, and, of course, her great friend, Knightley.

The day so far, in Emma's mind, had not been a success. Frank Churchill had hardly spoken a word to Harriet, despite Emma's efforts to nudge them into conversation together, and Mr Knightley was quieter than usual. Mrs Elton was insulted that no one had complimented her fashionably large bonnet, and Jane Fairfax looked very ill and irritable indeed, as though she'd rather be anywhere but there.

'Miss Woodhouse, what say you to that?' Frank asked, jolting her from her thoughts. She tore her eyes from Jane Fairfax's downcast expression.

'I was in a daydream,' Emma confessed. 'What was the question?'

'It was not a question, it was a statement.' He grinned. 'You shall choose me a wife! For I have decided I may go abroad and when I return, you shall have a wife waiting for me.'

'Is that so?'

'Yes. She must have hazel eyes and be as charming as you. In fact, you can spend the time I am abroad turning her into your double.'

Emma smiled, glancing at Harriet in the hope she was not offended by his compliment to her. But Harriet was busy taking a strawberry from the basket offered to her by Mr Knightley and had not noticed.

Glancing round the picnic blanket, Frank Churchill leaned in to whisper in Emma's ear.

'Our companions are determined not to have fun today. What can we do to rouse them?'

'Let us leave them to their thoughts,' Emma replied quietly. 'They do not have to ruin our day.'

'Indeed, Miss Woodhouse, but you know that I must be entertained, and I shall not put up with excessively stupid company who do not speak!' He grinned broadly before raising his voice and addressing the group. 'Miss Woodhouse has ordered me to ask you what you are all thinking?'

Mr Knightley raised his eyebrows. 'Is that really what Miss Woodhouse would like?'

'Oh no!' she cried, laughing at Frank. 'I did not wish it, nor order any such thing.'

Mrs Elton cleared her throat pointedly. 'Yes, well, if anyone should order anything, I should think it would be *me*, as the organiser of the party.'

She turned to look at her husband so that he could agree, but accidentally hit him in the face with her fashionably large bonnet.

'Ladies and gentlemen,' Frank continued, 'Miss Woodhouse demands to be entertained and so it shall be so.'

Emma shook her head, smiling at his silliness.

'Let us start the game – she demands that each person here say three things,' he explained. 'One clever statement and two dull ones; *or* two clever statements and one dull one; *or* three things very dull indeed! And Miss Woodhouse shall laugh heartily at them all!'

'Oh, what a fun game!' Miss Bates cried, giggling before saying in a self-deprecating and good-humoured manner, 'And how fortunate that we are allowed to say three dull things. For I shall be sure to say three dull things, like I always do!'

Emma could not resist.

'There may indeed be a difficulty for you, Miss Bates,' she replied, 'for you will be limited to say *only* three dull things.'

There was silence. Frank Churchill attempted to suppress a snigger.

Miss Bates turned red and her eyes fell to the ground. 'Oh yes. Yes, I see what you mean. I will try to hold my tongue. I must be very dull indeed, very disagreeable. For Miss Woodhouse would never say such a thing to an old friend, unless I was very disagreeable indeed.'

After a moment of awkwardness, the party continued with the game but Emma was aware that Mr Knightley was staring at her in great disapproval. He then stood up abruptly and asked Miss Bates if she would do him the honour of walking with him. Emma did not think any more about it until the end of the day when Mr Knightley accompanied her to her carriage.

'Emma, how could you?' he snapped when they were out of everyone's hearing.

Emma was struck by his tone, frowning in confusion.

'How could you be so unfeeling to Miss Bates?' he continued, shaking his head in disgust. 'I did not think you had the ability to be so cold.'

'What?' Emma would have laughed if he had not looked so serious. 'How could I help saying what I did? Everyone was thinking it! I doubt she even understood my meaning.'

'Yes, she did. She has not stopped talking about it. She feels it greatly. She keeps saying how good you are to put up with her all these years, how embarrassed she is to be so dull, how irksome she must be for us all.'

'She knows I think well of her! But she is also ridiculous, you must agree.'

'Emma,' Mr Knightley said, in so disapproving a tone that Emma's cheeks began to grow hot with shame, 'I would allow you to mock her for being ridiculous if she was wealthy and comfortable like you. But she is poor. And she will only get poorer as she gets older. She deserves your compassion! Your friendship! She is so kind and adoring of you. She has watched you grow up and felt honoured to have your notice. And for you to laugh at her and to humble her in front of all her friends! And not just that, but in front of those who are guided by you in your treatment of others.'

They had reached the carriage. Emma did not know what to say. His words stung her greatly and she hung her head in shame. She hadn't thought about it like that and she felt mortified. She wished she could apologise at once to dear Miss Bates, who had never been anything but goodness itself.

Mr Knightley hesitated, noticing her hurt expression.

'I only say all this to you, Emma, because I am your friend. I *know* that you are kinder and better than how you have acted today. I hope that you can do yourself greater justice in the future.'

He offered his hand to help her into the carriage and, with a bow of his head, left her. Her carriage jolted forwards, setting off towards Hartfield, and Emma began to cry as, through the carriage window, she watched Mr Knightley walk angrily away from her.

CHAPTER TWENTY

Emma felt terrible. Worse than terrible.

She had a sleepless night, distraught at her actions and unable to get Mr Knightley's disappointed expression out of her mind. She made a promise to herself to make a great effort with Miss Bates from now on.

She called on her first thing the next morning and was relieved to find that Miss Bates was as kind and cheery as ever. She was of a forgiving nature and Miss Woodhouse was so deeply affectionate towards her, the incident would readily be forgotten.

Emma returned to Hartfield feeling hopeful,

but all good feeling disappeared when she found Mr Knightley waiting for her.

'I am going to London,' he said in a serious tone. 'I wanted to say goodbye.'

'This is very sudden,' she replied, a lump rising in her throat. 'I hope that ... I hope it is not anything here that has prompted your leaving.'

'I have been thinking of visiting my brother for some time.'

He took her hand and went to kiss it, before stopping suddenly, letting her hand go. Emma held back tears. He had never hesitated before. He must be disgusted by her.

Mr Knightley stayed in London for days and Emma was troubled by his absence. She was out in the garden one morning, thinking about him and how she might make amends for her behaviour, when Mr Weston arrived in a matter of urgency, begging that she come to his house at once.

'What is the matter?' Emma asked Mrs Weston,

as she walked into her friend's drawing room. 'Mr Weston would not say a word on the way over here.'

'Oh, Emma.' Mrs Weston looked pale and upset. 'We have some news. Mrs Churchill has passed away.'

'Oh! I am so sorry,' Emma said dutifully. 'I hope that Frank—'

'That is not the news that I mean to tell you, however.' Mrs Weston continued. She looked down at her hands as she searched for the right words. 'Mrs Churchill's death has meant that ... Frank can reveal a truth. A truth that has shocked us to the core. A truth that I fear may hurt others deeply.'

'Mrs Weston, do tell me what the matter is,' Emma pleaded, distressed at seeing her friend so anxious. 'Let me comfort you.'

'Frank Churchill is engaged to Jane Fairfax.'

Emma stared at her, unsure if she'd heard her correctly.

'They have been secretly engaged for months,'

Mrs Weston continued. 'Ever since they met at Weymouth.'

Emma leapt to her feet in horror. 'You are not serious! Frank Churchill and … Jane Fairfax? *Engaged*? To be married! You must be mistaken!'

'My dear Emma, it is true,' Mrs Weston said, averting her eyes from Emma's. 'They did not tell a soul. Frank knew his aunt would never allow it to go ahead. Now that she has passed away, he is free to announce it. I hardly believe it. I thought I knew him. I thought I knew' – she looked at Emma, pained – 'I thought I knew how he felt.'

Emma slowly took her seat again. She was in a state of shock. He had been engaged to Jane Fairfax all this time. Before he'd even met Emma. *How could this be?*

'Emma, the news of this secret engagement has hurt myself and his father deeply. We cannot pretend that his behaviour here in Highbury has been in any way forgivable. We are so worried of *whom else* it may hurt.'

Emma understood what she was saying and spoke quickly so as to put her friend out of misery. 'Mrs Weston, let me reassure you. There was a time when I thought I liked Frank Churchill. But

I was wrong. He is only a friend, nothing more to me, and that is the truth.'

Mrs Weston looked as though the weight of the world had been lifted from her shoulders. She jumped to her feet and embraced Emma with tears of joy.

On her walk home, Emma had the time to ponder this startling, most unexpected news. Frank Churchill had behaved in an appalling manner. He had deceived them all at great cost. Not only had he been in danger of hurting Emma, but he must have injured Jane Fairfax by flirting with Emma in such a way in front of her! No wonder Jane had been looking so ill! How mortifying for Emma now to think back on their theories about Mr Dixon and Jane! The mysterious pianoforte must have been sent from Frank.

And what of Harriet? Another blow to her heart! Oh, this was all so dreadful! Emma recalled the time he spoke to her at Hartfield, when he said he had something important to tell her before he left. It must have been his secret engagement. If he had only told her then and saved so much pain and embarrassment! She reached home to find Harriet waiting for her and Emma felt sick that she would have to tell her.

'Miss Woodhouse, have you heard?' Harriet asked at once. 'Frank Churchill secretly engaged to Miss Fairfax! How odd! Did you have any idea of it?'

Emma was surprised at how well she had taken the news. She did not look grieved in the slightest.

'I had no idea at all. Dear Harriet, if I had, I never would have encouraged your feelings.'

Harriet frowned in confusion. 'My feelings? Whatever do my feelings have to do with it?'

'Your feelings for Mr Frank Churchill.'

Harriet laughed in surprise. 'Miss Woodhouse, I have never had any feelings for Mr Frank Churchill!'

'But, the superior gentleman you spoke of'

– Emma blinked at her – 'you ... you said that your feelings grew from when he rescued you ...'

'Oh I see.' Harriet shook her head, smiling. 'But there has been a mistake here. You thought I was speaking of Mr Frank Churchill rescuing me from the travellers! No, no, Miss Woodhouse, I wasn't talking about Mr Frank Churchill. I was talking of Mr Knightley.'

Emma stared at her, before whispering, '*Mr Knightley?*'

'Yes, Mr Knightley! He rescued me at the ball. That's what I was talking of.'

'You ... you are in love with ... Mr Knightley.' Emma sat down in shock. 'Good God.'

Emma's heart was thudding hard against her

chest and she suddenly found it hard to breathe. Harriet watched her, oblivious to any discomfort.

'Harriet,' Emma said eventually, so quietly that Harriet had to come closer to hear her, 'do you think that Mr Knightley returns your feelings?'

Harriet nodded. 'Yes, Miss Woodhouse. I had not dared to imagine that my feelings might be returned, but then you told me to let my feelings be guided by his actions, and I've noticed he has been paying me a lot of attention.' She paused, smiling gratefully. 'It is all thanks to you, Miss Woodhouse.'

Emma listened to Harriet in forced calmness. She sat for a few minutes in silence until Harriet prompted an opinion. Emma was able to offer her a weak smile and earnestly admit that Mr Knightley would never show he had feelings for her unless he really did.

Harriet was delighted by the answer and left Hartfield cheerful, longing for Mr Knightley's return.

EMMA

Emma felt wretched. She sat in despair, tears flowing down her cheeks. Harriet's declaration had served to bring forth a truth in Emma that she had not realised until now. A truth that had struck through her heart with the speed of an arrow.

Emma was in love with Mr Knightley.

The feeling was so overwhelming, so powerful that she could hardly breathe. *She was in love with Mr Knightley.* Her wonderful, perfect, closest friend. Emma closed her eyes, pained at the unfairness of it all.

She had grown to love him so dearly, only to lose him for ever.

CHAPTER TWENTY-ONE

She had been so blind.

Emma sighed, sitting at the window the next morning and looking out at the rain. How could she have been so mistaken? She had been wrong about everybody, most of all herself. She could not bear the thought of losing Mr Knightley. And what must he think of her? He, who knew all of her faults and weaknesses. He could not love her, surely. But how would Emma bear seeing him with Harriet? She could not!

Her mind was racing with memories. She thought of Mr Knightley at the ball. How she had only had eyes for him. She remembered how happy she'd felt when they danced together, happier than she had ever been before. She considered how outraged she'd been at the thought of his being matched with Jane Fairfax. She had been repulsed, horrified at the idea of his loving and marrying someone else. How could she have not recognised her feelings before? She had become so complacent with his friendship. She was so used to being *first* with him in everything. Now, would she be second to Harriet Smith in his eyes?

She was in such pain that as soon as she saw the rain had stopped, she stood up and went to go for a walk around the garden. She couldn't sit any longer. She took a turn about the lawn, breathing in the fresh air, hoping that the outdoors might lift her spirits. She reminded herself that she had always said she would never marry, but that only made her feel worse. How alone she would feel without him at Hartfield.

A gentleman came through the garden door

and began walking towards her. She stopped suddenly on seeing who it was.

'Mr Knightley,' she said, greeting him. She did not know where to look. So strong and overwhelming were her feelings for him, that she half suspected he might be able to see them if he looked directly into her eyes.

'Emma,' he replied, looking agitated. 'How do you do?'

'How was London? How is my sister and your brother?'

'They are both well.'

'And the children?'

'Very well.'

'When did you return from London?'

'This morning.'

'You must have got caught in the rain!'

'I did.'

There was silence and then Mr Knightley gestured to the path.

'Might I join you on your walk?'

'Please.'

He fell into step with her. Emma was in a state of agitation. She could not think how to act around him. He was acting strangely, too. He was tense and unsure. A thought struck her that filled her with dread: he might want to tell her of his feelings for Harriet. She did not have the strength to hear it.

'There was been some news while you were away,' Emma said, hoping to distract him. 'The very best kind of news. A wedding.'

'If you are speaking of Frank Churchill and Miss Fairfax, I am aware of it.'

'Oh!' Emma hesitated. 'It has come as quite a surprise; I had no suspicions of the attachment. I seem to be doomed to blindness.'

At this, Mr Knightley stopped and took Emma's hand in his. Just at his touch, her heart sped up, thudding hard against her chest.

'Emma,' he said gently, 'time will heal your

wound. Frank Churchill is a scoundrel. He is a disgrace to the name of man.'

'Mr Knightley,' Emma said hurriedly, hoping he would not drop her hand any time soon; it felt so warm clasped over hers, 'I have no wound to speak of. I know what you must think, but I have never had any feelings for Mr Frank Churchill.'

Mr Knightley's eyes searched Emma's. 'Is that true?'

'Yes. He has done me no harm. I have no doubt of their being happy together.'

Mr Knightley nodded, deep in thought. He let go of her hand and they continued their walk a few moments in silence before he spoke again.

'I believe I envy Frank Churchill. I envy his situation.'

Emma was struck with horror. By this sentence, his intentions became clear. He was thinking of marriage and was about to talk of proposing to Harriet.

EMMA

Mr Knightley glanced at Emma, who did not say or do anything but stare ahead.

'Are you not going to ask me why I envy an engagement?' Mr Knightley pointed out nervously. 'Well, I am going to tell you anyway. Though I may wish I'd never said it.'

'Then don't speak it! Don't speak it!' Emma cried in anguish, forgetting herself.

Mr Knightley was mortified and silenced by this reaction. His eyes fell to the floor and he increased his pace so that he walked ahead. Emma shook her head at herself. Again, she was at fault. If he needed to confide in her, then she could not stop him from doing so.

'Mr Knightley, forgive me,' she said, hurrying to catch him up. 'I stopped you ungraciously just now and gave you pain. If you wish to speak to me as a friend, then please do. As your friend, I cannot and will not stop you.'

'As my friend?' Mr Knightley repeated, before

sighing and turning to face her. 'That is how you wish us to stay. As friends. But Emma' – he paused and then lifted his eyes to meet hers – 'might I ever have hope to be something more to you?'

She was too startled to speak. Too afraid of having misheard him or mistaken his meaning.

'You know I'm not good at speeches,' he continued, in a voice she had never heard him use before. It was so earnest and gentle. He paused and then said softly, 'Perhaps, if I loved you less, I might be able to talk about it more.'

Emma gasped. Was this happening? Was she dreaming it?

'Did you never guess why I didn't like Frank Churchill, even before I'd met him?' Mr Knightley continued anxiously, unsure as to how his words were being received. 'I knew he was intended for *you*. I could not bear to watch you together. I, who had loved you for so long. After the picnic at Box Hill, I went to London in the hopes of getting you out of my head. But I saw you everywhere I looked and longed to just be near you. When I heard of Frank Churchill's engagement, I felt ... I thought there might be some *hope*. I rode through the rain back to you. Just to be near you. To hear your voice again.' He stepped closer to her. 'Emma, is there a way ... Might I have hope of gaining your affection one day?'

'Mr Knightley,' Emma began, feeling as though she might burst with happiness, 'I have been silent because I have been too afraid to speak and awaken from this dream. I was convinced that you could not feel this way, when I have too many faults to deserve you!'

'Deserve me?' he said, taking her hands and holding them tight. 'I have lectured you and blamed you and ... I have hardly dared to hope that I might one day deserve *you*, the best and sweetest person I have ever met. I can assure you that, to me, any faults of yours only serve to make you more perfect.'

Emma smiled up at him, her eyes filling with tears of joy.

'Emma,' he said, a hopeful smile creeping across his face, 'will you marry me?'

CHAPTER TWENTY–TWO

The engagement of Mr Knightley to Miss Emma Woodhouse brought much joy to Highbury.

Emma had a moment of panic when she realised she would have to leave her father, which he would never allow, but Mr Knightley offered a perfect and surprising solution – that instead of Emma moving to his estate, Donwell Abbey, on the marriage, Mr Knightley would live at Hartfield with Emma and her father.

Mr Woodhouse was, therefore, able to celebrate the news. For he could not love a son-in-law better than Mr Knightley, and, what's more, he had heard that Mrs Weston's poultry house had recently been broken into and all her turkeys stolen! It made him uneasy that there might be a thief about the place, and he was very much looking forward to having Mr Knightley in the house to protect them.

Mr and Mrs Weston rejoiced in such happy news, both wondering how they hadn't predicted the match before. Mr Weston talked so much about how well-suited they were, that he soon convinced himself he *had* in fact foreseen it and told everyone else so, too.

Emma visited Jane Fairfax and both had been able to congratulate the other. Now that her engagement was public and all confusion explained, Jane was no longer reserved, but cheerful and warm.

She was terribly apologetic to Miss Woodhouse. She had been purposefully cold to her, believing Frank might have feelings for Miss Woodhouse and betray his promise. Emma was equally as sorry – she had not been a friend to Jane as she should have been, jealous of her superior beauty and talent. They laughed about it together and it had been warmly decided that they would be great friends from now on.

There was one person that Emma had not seen since the engagement was announced, and there was not a minute of the day that Emma did not think about her. Harriet Smith was yet to come to Hartfield.

'I have some news for you, Emma,' Mr Knightley said one morning. Since their engagement, Mr Knightley and Emma had spent as much time as possible together. She did not want to spend one day apart from him again.

'Good news or bad news?'

He hesitated. 'I am not sure.'

'I can see you are trying not to smile, Mr Knightley,' she laughed. 'And so I can safely assume it is good news.'

'I think it good news, but I fear you may think it bad news. It's about your friend, Harriet Smith.'

'Harriet?' Emma asked, feeling her stomach

drop. 'What of her?'

'She is engaged to be married to Robert Martin.'

Emma started. 'No! It's . . . impossible!'

'I heard it from Robert Martin himself. He came to tell me this very morning.' He studied her expression. 'You are unhappy at the news?'

'No! No, I . . . are you sure? Are you quite sure that Robert Martin and Harriet are engaged? He has proposed and she has accepted?'

'Quite sure.'

'Really? Because, you know, Robert Martin often talks to you about business and cows and things. Perhaps you got muddled?'

Mr Knightley stared at her. 'Do you think I am a blockhead? I am quite sure that when he talks to me about cows, I know he is talking about cows, and when he talks to me about being engaged, I can understand that he is engaged!'

'How did the engagement come about?'

'I will let Miss Smith tell you herself.'

'I would very much like to know now!'

'Precisely.' Mr Knightley smiled, nodding to the window. 'I can see her coming up the drive. I'm sure she'd like to give you all the particulars.'

Emma leapt to her feet and rushed from the room to greet her friend at the front door.

'Harriet!' she cried, embracing her. 'It is so good to see you!'

'Oh, Miss Woodhouse.' Harriet blushed, not sure how to start. 'I ... well ... I must offer you congratulations and ... admit that on my part, there is some embarrassment.'

'Harriet, please do not make yourself uneasy.' Emma smiled warmly. 'I have been longing to talk to you and tell you how sorry I am for everything.'

'Do not apologise to me, Miss Woodhouse! I must tell you that the feelings I confessed to you of late were not right. In that, I misread myself. If that makes sense. I was silly and I deceived myself and' – she gave a small smile – 'I hope you can forgive me.'

'Harriet, there is nothing to forgive.' Emma paused, every anxiety she'd had for Harriet washing away, replaced by exulting happiness. 'Mr Martin visited Mr Knightley this morning and I would like to offer you my warmest and sincerest congratulations!'

Harriet could not hide her pleasure. Any embarrassment was forgotten as she began to tell Miss Woodhouse her story. Mr Martin had met her at a party recently. They had spoken as if they had never been apart. They then sat together at dinner the following evening. It was there that Mr Martin proposed and Harriet accepted.

She'd realised that she had loved him all along.

'I have to say, Mr E,' Mrs Elton said to her husband at the wedding of Mr and Mrs Knightley, 'when it comes to the bridal gown, there is a shocking lack of white satin! This is because I was not consulted on such matters, you know.'

Mr Elton agreed with his wife as they joined the host of guests following the couple out of the church. Miss Bates was ahead of them telling Jane Fairfax and Frank Churchill that she had never seen so happy a couple at the altar in all her days. Mrs Harriet Martin was breathlessly gushing to Mrs Weston about how beautiful Mrs Knightley looked in her gown, while Mr Martin was busy congratulating Mr Weston on the birth of their little girl. Mr Woodhouse was with Mr Perry, the village apothecary, boasting of his new son-in-law and assuring him that he had taken great pains to ensure the cake served at the wedding reception would be sliced in very small pieces, so that the guests were not in any danger.

At the front of the procession, Mr Knightley stopped to draw Emma towards him.

'Well then, *my* Emma,' he began, smiling playfully at her, 'what do you think of this Highbury match? Is it a good one?'

Her eyes sparkled up at him. 'Despite its many imperfections, I must say I believe this match to be quite perfect. Quite perfect, indeed.'

And as Mr Knightley leant down to kiss her, Emma knew that their happy union heralded the end of her matchmaking days.

She would not miss them.

A NOTE FROM KATY

Adapting Jane Austen's *Emma* has been my ultimate dream project.

I fell head-over-heels in love with Jane Austen's world in 1995, when I was seven years old, and my family sat down together to watch the BBC television adaptation of *Pride and Prejudice*. When I was a few years older, I tackled her novels for the first time. That was when the obsession really started.

JANE AUSTEN

Jane Austen is, without a doubt, my favourite author. I have shelves devoted to many, many different editions of her novels, along with any book ever written about her and her life. I also have a framed photograph on one of those bookshelves of me wearing a bonnet, standing in front of her house. (Side note: I do not look good in a bonnet.)

The thing is, everyone knows that Jane was very clever, very funny and very talented, but what is sometimes brushed over is that she was also very BRAVE.

Back then, women had no power and were expected to look pretty, marry well and not do much else. They weren't supposed to have a proper education. They weren't supposed to have opinions, to know anything about politics or to sit around reading. And they *certainly* weren't supposed to waste their time writing novels.

But Jane didn't let that stop her. It wasn't easy,

but with a lot of determination and hard work, she became a published writer. That took guts. She's now one of the most famous and influential authors of all time.

And long may her bonnet reign.

A NOTE FROM ÉGLANTINE

My name is Églantine Ceulemans, and as you might have noticed thanks to my first name . . . I am French!

In France, we tend to associate Britain with wonderful English gardens, a unique sense of humour, William Shakespeare and, last but not least, Jane Austen!

It was such an honour to have the opportunity

to illustrate Jane Austen's stories. I have always enjoyed reading books that are filled with love, laughter and happy endings, and Austen writes all of those things brilliantly. And who wouldn't love to illustrate gorgeous dresses, stunning mansions and passionate young women standing up for their deep convictions? I also tried to do justice to Austen's humour and light-heartedness by drawing characterful people and adding in friendly pets (sometimes well-hidden and always witnessing intense but mostly funny situations!).

I discovered Jane Austen's work with *Pride and Prejudice* one sun-filled summer, and I have such good memories of sitting reading it in the garden beneath my grandmother's weeping willow. This setting definitely helped me to fall in love with the book, but it would be a lie to say that I wasn't moved by Elizabeth and Mr Darcy's love story and that I didn't laugh when her mother tried (with no shame at all) to marry her daughters to all the best catches in the town! I imagined all those characters in my head so vividly, and it was a real pleasure to finally illustrate them, alongside all Austen's other amazing characters.

Jane Austen is an author who managed to depict nineteenth-century England with surprising modernity. She questioned the morality of so-called well-to-do people and she managed to write smartly, sharply and independently, at time where women were considered to be nothing if not married to a man. I hope that these illustrated versions of her books will help you to question the past *and* the present, without ever forgetting to laugh ... and to dream!

SO, WHO WAS JANE AUSTEN?

Jane Austen was born in 1775 and had seven siblings. Her parents were well-respected in their local community, and her father was the clergyman for a nearby parish. She spent much of her life helping to run the family home, whilst reading and writing in her spare time.

* JANE AUSTEN *

Jane began to anonymously publish her work in her thirties and four of her novels were released during her lifetime: *Sense and Sensibility*, *Pride and Prejudice*, *Mansfield Park* and *Emma*. However, at the age of forty-one she became ill, eventually dying in 1817. Her two remaining novels, *Northanger Abbey* and *Persuasion*, were published after her death.

Austen's books are well-known for their comedy, wit and irony. Her observations about wealthy society, and especially the role women played in it, were unlike anything that had been published before. Her novels were not widely read or praised until years later, but they have gone on to leave a mark on the world for ever, inspiring countless poems, books, plays and films.

AND WHAT WAS IT LIKE IN 1815?

WHAT JOBS DID MEN DO?

Men's social status determined the jobs available to them. Very wealthy men usually spent their time overseeing the land that they owned. Men from the upper or middle classes could be lawyers, doctors, army officers or work for the church or government. Lower-class men might be labourers, soldiers or miners. Being a farmer – such as Mr Martin – was a respectable profession, but people from the upper classes, such as Emma, sometimes looked down on farmers, believing it was not an aristocratic job.

WHAT JOBS DID WOMEN DO?

Women had very little choice when it came to work. They were most often factory workers, servants, chaperones or governesses. Women's lives were often determined by the type of man they were able to marry, which explains why Emma is so keen for her friend Harriet to marry well. At the beginning of the book, Emma does not believe she needs to marry but this is very unusual for the era as most women did not have a fortune of their own.

WHAT WAS A GOVERNESS?

A governess was a woman who was employed to teach children at home. Only the very wealthy could afford to have a governess. The fact that Emma had a governess – Miss Taylor – shows that her family had plenty of money! Women who were educated themselves but did not expect to be able to marry a wealthy man often considered becoming a governess, as it was one of the few respectable middle-class career options available to them. Many of the characters who live in Highbury expect that Miss Jane Fairfax will become a governess.

WHAT WAS SCHOOL LIKE?

School wasn't compulsory until 1880. Before this, only well-off families could afford to send their children to school because it cost money to do so. Girls and boys were always educated at separate schools. The school that Miss Harriet Smith works at would have been for a small number of girls, and they would have lived there during term time. Children from poor families often had to work from a young age on farms, in factories and as servants, rather than receiving an education.

COLLECT THEM ALL!

AWESOMELY AUSTEN

JANE AUSTEN'S
SENSE AND SENSIBILITY

WITTY WORDS BY JOANNA NADIN
DELIGHTFUL DOODLES BY ÉGLANTINE CEULEMANS

AWESOMELY AUSTEN

JANE AUSTEN'S
MANSFIELD PARK

WITTY WORDS BY AYISHA MALIK
DELIGHTFUL DOODLES BY ÉGLANTINE CEULEMANS

AWESOMELY AUSTEN

JANE AUSTEN'S
NORTHANGER ABBEY

WITTY WORDS BY STEVEN BUTLER
DELIGHTFUL DOODLES BY ÉGLANTINE CEULEMANS